Billy's Blues

Billy's Blues

by

C. Rips Meltzer

THE PERMANENT PRESS
SAG HARBOR, NY 11963

Library of Congress Cataloging-in-Publication Data

Meltzer, C. Rips.
    Billy's Blues / by C. Rips Meltzer.
        p.   cm.
    ISBN 1-57962-005-1
    I. Title.
    PS35633.E44965B55   1998
    813'.54--dc21   97-21537
                                   CIP

THE PERMANENT PRESS
4170 Noyac Road
Sag Harbor, NY 11963

To my mother, Beatrice,
without whose support
this book would never
have been written.

The Ballad of Billy the Kid

I'll sing you a true song of Billy the Kid,
I'll sing of the desperate deeds that he did,
Way out in New Mexico, long, long ago,
When a man's only chance was his own forty-four.

When Billy the Kid was a very young lad
In old Silver City he went to the bad;
Way out in the West with a gun in his hand
At the age of twelve years he did kill his first man.

Fair Mexican maidens play guitars and sing
A song of *El Chivato*, their boy bandit king.
How ere his young manhood had reached its sad end
With a notch on his pistol for twenty-one men.

`Twas on the same night that poor Billy died
He said to his friends: "I'm not satisfied.
There are twenty-one men I have put bullets through
And Sheriff Pat Garrett must make twenty-two."

Now this is how Billy the Kid met his fate.
The bright moon was shining, the hour was late.
Cut down by Pat Garrett, who once was his friend,
the young outlaw's life had now come to its end.

There's many a young man with face fine and fair
Who starts out in life with a chance to be square,
But just like poor Billy he wanders astray,
And loses his life in the very same way.

Reverend Andrew Jenkins

THE FIVE CENT
WIDE AWAKE
LIBRARY

Entered according to Act of Congress, in the year 1881, by FRANK TOUSEY, in the office of the Librarian of Congress, at Washington, D. C.

Entered at the Post Office at New York, N. Y., as Second Class Matter.

No. 451. | COMPLETE. | FRANK TOUSEY, Publisher, 20 Rose Street, N. Y. New York, August 29, 1881. Issued Every Monday. | PRICE 5 CENTS. | Vol. I.

THE TRUE LIFE OF BILLY THE KID

Book One

★

The East

A system of hypocrisy,
which lasts through whole years
is one seldom satisfactorily practiced
by a person one-and-twenty.

Thackeray, *Vanity Fair*

Chapter One

The evening begins like every other day. A setting sun filters softly between black curtains as I roll over, curl up, and pull covers warmly overhead. Surrounded by a bevy of plump pillows, I happily await the best sleep, the kind of sleep that can only be enjoyed after alarm clocks have long been silenced and forgotten. Ten minutes here. Five minutes there. Diving quickly into the most vivid of dreams, sinking slowly to the bottom, rushing the surface for air before submerging into another breathless vision—each complete conception may last but minutes or mere seconds, yet each details more than could ever be captured with language, paint or song. Such dreams were believed by the ancient Greeks to predict the future.

Each salubrious plunge is so consuming that even bodily pain withdraws, and I hate pain. Some men are built for speed, others brute force. I am built for comfort. Where others have muscle, I have cushioning. Some talk of scars earned on battlefields or in sports arenas, but the only injuries I seem to acquire occur in bed. I wake with pulled muscles, jammed fingers, and sprained ankles among an assortment of other ills.

But my sufferings begin long before the first battle with sleep. Early skirmishes involve just trying to get comfortable. Those whose bodies were built for comfort often have the most difficulty in finding it. Lying upon my belly, my prodigious girth forces the spine to curve outward. This results in searing back spasms. Belly up, my knees buckle under gravity's strain. On the side, my shoulders groan beneath the heavy load and the only way to keep these copious thighs from crushing my little he-biddies is to wedge a firm pillow forcibly between the knees. Not until sunrise, with curtains drawn and earplugs inserted, does the night's war of attrition leave me exhausted enough to trust the tremulous arms of Morpheus as he carries me away with noiseless wings to land of slumber.

For me, however, it's a flight filled with turbulence. After a day of fitful sleep, the sun finally sets and twilight tucks the earth to bed. Not until then can the final aphoristic magic begin. Freed from the prying eyes of Helios yet still safe from the danger of night, I'm granted a last episodic respite before the painful moment of resurrection.

Stuffing an extra pillow between the knees, I dream on . . .

Floating beneath the stars on a cloudless night, my weightless spirit glides above a dark green forest touched lightly by the moon. A soft radiance flickers ahead, a campfire. I zero in to see a blanketed figure sleeping before the glow. Familiar in its curves, I realize that the slumbering body is mine, which I find peculiar, because I've never slept outside so exposed to the dangerous elements of the natural world. Stranger still is the camp: a rustic pot hung above the blaze from a triangle of sticks, two horses tied to a tree, and two unfurled bedrolls, one empty. Looking down upon the ugly lump that was once myself, I feel peaceful. The cares that once possessed me when embodied seem as trite as they were infinite: the need for rest, clean clothes, warmth, Hershey's chocolate. Satisfying the endless needs of the body, especially such a spacious one, was an undertaking of Sysiphian proportions. Now, outside the body, I feel unfettered by such corporeal torments.

Then I notice a tall shadow at the edge of woods on the other side of the fire. The dark figure stands perfectly still like a Cimmerian sorcerer. Finally, the shade steps into the circle of light. A wide-brimmed sombrero hides his face. Wearing cowboy boots and denim trousers over wiry bowlegs, he cradles something beneath a thick poncho. As he steps around the flames, a flash of light reveals the barrel of a rifle. He walks up to my sleeping figure and flips the left side of the poncho over his shoulder freeing the rifle butt. He lowers the barrel and points it toward my body. From deep in the woods a sound is heard. Startled, he raises the gun.

"Hello?"

The voice sounds old and frail.

"Hello... Hello...?"

All space and time ceases. Everything becomes this voice from outside our circle of light. Its volume rises and like a blind man stumbling forward, it comes closer, aged, painful, a voice cracking with loneliness and confusion, seeking me, beckoning for me to answer:

"Hello... Hello... Hello...?"

Icy fingers reach beneath moist sheets. Faraway sounds seep in through earplugs: a distant train, a car alarm. All aches awaken and pound for recognition: ankles, knees, back, neck, an overwhelming need to relieve myself. The voice repeats itself, closer, vivid, plaintive.

"Hello... Hello... Hello...?"

Heartbeats stab my chest. My eyes open to darkness. Reaching for the answering machine, I turn the volume down and the voice trails off into peaceful emptiness. I slip off the slumber mask, remove earplugs, and check the clock.

It's 6:30 p.m. Night has settled upon the Northeast. I'm up. Now what?

Chapter Two

After years of searching and months of waiting, I finally received today, via the mail, an ultra-rare, original copy of the most underrated book in the 20th century, *The Saga of Billy the Kid*. It was the first legitimate biography of the most famous outlaw in the late 19th century Southwest, yet, by the time Walter Noble Burns wrote *The Saga of Billy the Kid* in 1925, the career of America's first child criminal had been long forgotten by a country caught up in the turbulent twenties. By the depression thirties, however, the country was ready again for outlaw legends. That's when Metro-Goldwyn-Mayer Pictures got hold of Burns' *Saga* and made the immensely popular film, *Billy The Kid*.

The *Kid* was never forgotten again.

> He reached out his manacled hands to place his wager of ten matches when, seemingly by accident, he brushed the jack of hearts off on to the floor at Bell's left side. "Didn't mean to do that, Bell," the young boy apologized. "Hard to play with handcuffs on like this."
>
> "That's all right, Kid," replied Assistant Deputy J.W. Bell. "I'll get it."
>
> Bell bent over to pick up the card. Holding the deck in his left hand, he reached for the card with his right. To do so, he had to turn slightly away from the table. For a fraction of a second his head dipped below the level of the top, his eyes intent upon the card on the floor.
>
> It was Billy the Kid's chance in a million for which he had been waiting weeks with the deadly patience of a panther.[1]

Billy the Kid: notorious boy bandit of the wild and woolly West. It was said that he killed a man for every year of his life, "twenty-one," according to old-timers, "not including Mexicans and Indians." *Billy the Kid*: his bold escape from the Lincoln County Jail, just days before he was due to hang by the neck until dead, ranks as one of the most infamous escapes in America's history right up there with John Dillinger's gun carved out of wood and Ted Bundy's leap from a second floor court library window. *Billy the Kid*: hunted down and killed with a proverbial shot in the dark by Sheriff Pat F. Garrett, the man who once was his friend.

> As Bell stooped, the butt of his six-shooter projected within reach of the Kid's hand. Leaning across the table, the Kid snatched the weapon. When Bell raised his head, he was looking into the muzzle of his own gun.[2]

Billy the Kid: the tragic figure was born Henry Michael McCarty, November 20, 1859, fatherless, in the poverty-stricken, disease-infested Irish Fourth Ward of Lower Manhattan where the World Trade Center stands today. *Billy the abandoned*: his loving mother, Catherine, migrated west with little Henry and brother Joe to drier air in a vain attempt to cure the tuberculosis that racked her once hardy frame only to leave Billy an orphan at the tender age of fourteen. *Little lost Billy*: thousands of miles from familiar city streets, he was forced to live under a slave-driving step-father who had gained rights to the child through an arranged marriage bartered by a desperate Catherine in Santa Fe shortly before her death. *Ill-fated Billy*: he was driven into a life of crime after being duped into hiding stolen laundry by Sombrero Jack, a local Fagin, in the dusty mining town of Silver City. Nobly refusing to snitch on his *compadre* (who had since skipped town leaving him to hold the bag, literally), Sheriff Harvey W. Whitehill jailed the young lad (his first trouble with the law), and promptly called a grand jury. The boy squeezed his wiry frame through the chimney of the city jail (his first of many escapes) and fled into the badlands of Arizona, a fugitive at the tender age of fifteen. Penniless and unarmed, *bad luck Billy* stumbled into Indian territory just south of the notorious Fort Apache.

> "What the hell, Kid!"
> "Do as I tell you, Bell, and be mighty quick about it," ordered the Kid in crisp, sharp tones. "Don't make a false move. You're a dead man if you do. I don't want to kill you. I'm not going to kill you. You've been good to me. Turn and walk out the door. I'm going to lock you in the armory."[3]

I take a spoonful of *Marshmallow Fluff*, a knifeful of *Skippy Roasted Honey Nut Peanut Butter,* and smear it onto slabs of *Hershey's Milk Chocolate*. Only four more portions await me, so I chew slowly, one square at a time, a little extra peanut butter where I can tolerate it, because I need protein for this herculean task of piecing together the life of this badly misappropriated and misused legend of the old Southwest.

> Bell faced about silently and marched out the door, the Kid, hampered by his leg irons, shuffling after him. As the deputy turned south in the hall, a sudden surge of anger, chagrin, hurt pride, swept through him. Why had he been such an easy dupe? Deaf to repeated warnings, he had been caught napping. He had fallen into a trap through which he should have seen with half an eye, a trap the Kid doubtless had been planning since their first card game together. This absurd situation was the upshot of his pity, his kindliness. He might have expected it. He had been a soft-hearted fool. What would Sheriff Pat Garrett think of him? What would that devil, Deputy Bob Olinger, say? Was there no way out of this? Desperate thoughts raced through his mind. Could he turn quickly and overpower the Kid? No. That seemed suicide. But if he could trick the Kid as the Kid had tricked him, he might yet save his reputation. Once out of the Kid's

clutches, he would organize the citizens and recapture or kill him. He came to the head of the back stairs just beyond which was the armory door. He shot a furtive glance over his shoulder. The Kid had fallen perhaps six feet behind him, making awkward progress, his ankle chains clattering. There were not more than a dozen steps from the upper floor to the point where the stairway turned. Once behind the angle of the wall, Bell would be safe. The stairs were his one forlorn hope. Swerving sharply, he plunged down. In one flying leap, he made the bend. His out-thrust hand struck the plastered wall; the heels of his cowboy boots cut splinters from the steps as he lunged for the shelter of the turn. One step more and the wall would shield him . . .[4]

A mere boy thrown into the world of men and what a world of men was life West of the Pecos. Angry Apaches violently defended the last of their homelands. Prowling gunfighters had free reign to act out an evil normally suppressed in civilized society. Roving bands of thieves plied their trade unhampered by law. But, far more dangerous, were the ruthless cattle barons who gobbled up the landscape before an encroaching civilization leaving many of the original settlers homeless, others dead. The resulting range wars forced the local citizenry to take sides or be cut down in the crossfire. It was a West filled with more perils and danger than any other epoch in American history. This notion of a mere child thrown into such a maelstrom, alone and without guidance, struggling to survive all while attempting to develop a code of conduct from which to behave—this was the essential conflict of the frontier. This manchild's *gestalt* symbolized the West's own struggle to merge into the modern, post-Civil War United States. Billy the Kid, coming of age in the very heart of the West at its wildest, was trying to manage a complex set of loose and ever-changing rules. Yet, a definitive code did exist. Arguments may have been settled with a gun, but they were settled *mano a mano.* Justice may have been at the end of a

17

rope, but it was swift, final, and unobscured by a sprawling legal system which, in urbanized centers, seemed to breed more crime than it solved. Yes, the West had its own code, but in a sense it was purer, simpler, more innocent compared to the complex set of rules from the older, corrupted East. The code of the West, however, was one the "civilized world" could not tolerate. Those who could not adapt to modernization were doomed. A new West stumbled out of the gunsmoke of the old—a West which would no longer tolerate the likes of its own prodigy, Billy the Kid, infant rascal, boy bandit king.

> The bullet struck Bell beneath the left shoulder blade, cut through his heart, and buried itself in the wall beyond.[5]

One crucial task in any research concerning an historical figure whose deeds have sprouted into unruly legend is to separate fiction from fact, myth from reality, story from history. No one has ever reported the authentic story of Henry Michael McCarty (*alias* Billy the Kid, Kid Antrim, William H. Bonney, *El Chivato*, or simply, The Kid). I can, because unlike the others, I have no reason to sway from the path of truthfulness. So far I've completed a weighty amount of research: books, periodicals, videos, tapes.

But facts can only go so far. I need to get a feel for how things really happened. I must close my eyes, think deeply, and meditate. I must allow his spirit to enter my body, putting myself in *his* shoes, understanding how *he* thought, and then stick a needle in my vein and use that blood for ink—except now it's *his* blood, the long dead blood of Billy the Kid. I'm speaking figuratively of course. I detest violence.

> Jamming Bell's six-shooter into his belt for emergencies, he stepped to the door of the armory, flung it open, and caught up Deputy Bob Olinger's double-barrel shotgun leaning against the wall.[6]

Another chocolate fluffer-nutter sandwich, cold milk to smooth the palate, and I ponder the first enticing mystery concerning Billy: the time he spent south of Fort Apache, in the land of the Chiricahua Apache. Led by the infamous Geronimo, these last "hostile" American Indians refused to be settled on the reservation where the land wasn't fit for crops or hunting. There, they would be left dependent on corrupt Indian agents who skimmed so much off the already meager rations that children and the old suffered from malnutrition and descended into coma-like stupors. While the women gave still-births, once-proud warriors grew listless, aroused only by the firewater which seemed created just for the purpose of making the Indian forget who he was.

Geronimo and his followers would undergo no such indignities. They roamed free within the so-called "Apache Triangle" unimpressed by the soldiers who wore pants with a yellow stripe. In full view of the guards from Fort Apache and Camps Thomas, Bowie, or Grant, the Apache boldly killed any yellow legs who strayed beyond the front gates.

"Garrett went over to White Oaks to-day to order the gallows," said Olinger. "Kid's getting scared. Dropped some talk this mornin' about makin' some kind of break. Broke open my double-barrelled shotgun and said, 'Each one of them shells is loaded with eighteen buckshot. Try to escape, I wish you would. I'd like to see you kickin' at a rope's end, but, when I come to think about it, I believe I'd rather murder you myself. Go ahead and make your break and you'll get eighteen buckshot between the shoulder blades."

Olinger downed the red liquor and ordered another three fingers. "But I'll get my revenge when the trap falls. I want to see him kick. Little devil. Hope he strangles a good longtime."

"That's the stuff," echoed Jimmy Dolan and J.G. Murphy.

They raised their glasses.

"Here's to the rope that chokes the life out of the little devil," said Olinger. Then a sudden crashing noise over in the courthouse startled them.[7]

It was through this desolate country—where water flowed only during the rainy season; where rattlesnakes, scorpions, and cougars ruled the nights, and renegade Apache patrolled the day lying in wait for invading settlers—it was in this land that Billy, then Henry Antrim, roamed. Two crucial years, from age fifteen to seventeen, lost to recorded history. What is known is this: as he walked through the gates of Camp Grant, bystanders wondered from where this strange boy had come. He dressed as a country jake wearing a derby, an oversized jacket, and matching pants rolled up to reveal clumsy city shoes.

> "When Henry Antrim came to Fort Thomas and asked for work, he said he was seventeen, though he didn't look to be a day past fourteen. Didn't know nothin' about horses, nothin' about cattle and could handle neither rope nor gun. We had trouble finding things for the boy to do, because he weren't no cowboy. Had to let him go though we gave'm money enough for a new set of clothes. Heard later he strayed over to Camp Grant.
> "Called him 'kid,' because he was so small: no taller than a mule, no heavier than a sack of flour. When they told me later that he was the Billy the Kid, the same one who fought in the Lincoln County War, I said, well doesn't that beat all. Must've grown some."[8]
> - W.J. 'Sorghum' Smith

Yes, he had wandered into the notorious Apache triangle as a boy, but came out two years later man enough to make his home among soldiers whose only relief from harsh army life was drinking, gambling, fighting and whoring. He also came out man enough to commit his first official murder deflating Windy Cahill, the camp blacksmith and bully, with a bullet in the stomach on the night of August 17, 1877.

I, Frank P. Cahill, being convinced that I am about to die, do make the following as my final statement: I was born in the county and town of Galway, Ireland. Yesterday, August 17th, 1877, I had some trouble with Henry Antrem, otherwise know as Kid, during which he shot me. I had called him a pimp, and he called me a son of a bitch, we then took hold of each other. I did not hit him, I think — saw him go for the pistol, and tried to get hold of it, but could not and he shot me in the belly. I have a sister named Margaret Flannigan living in East Cambridge, Mass. and another named Kate Conden, living in San Francisco. [9]

According to witnesses, Cahill had wrestled young Henry to the ground and began pummeling him with his thick fists. Half his weight, the boy reached for the blacksmith's own gun. He pulled the hammer back and squeezed the trigger while Cahill was in mid-punch. It was the first time the boy had ever fired a pistol.

Declared an "unjustifiable killing" by a grand jury, Henry was arrested, hand-cuffed, and thrown into the fort stockade which was filled with soldiers—traitors, deserters, and murderers of which he could now include himself, many of whom faced the firing squad. Civilians got the rope.

**Old enough to kill,
Old enough to hang.** [10]

A few nights later, as Captain G.C. Smith entertained guests in his quarters, shots rang out in the dark. It caused little excitement, but according to army procedure, the young Lieutenant Cheever, officer of the day, was sent out to investigate. He returned to inform Captain Smith that the sentries had fired upon one Henry Antrim, commonly referred to as 'the kid,' who had escaped into Apache country on 'Cashaw,' civilian John Murphy's racing pony. Awaiting orders, Lieutenant Cheever was surprised when the Captain simply offered him a fresh drink and told him to rejoin the party.

A week later a trader rode into camp with Cashaw. He said a runaway boy had asked him to return the pony to its rightful owner. Henry was on the run again, without horse or gun, but with outstanding warrants in both Arizona and New Mexico. An unwanted boy, yet a wanted man, Henry was now alone in the wilderness once again and unwelcome in both mining towns and forts. Forced into the life of a *desperado* there was only one place he knew of where outlaws were welcome. That was in the valley of the Pecos River, where men fought over cattle, land and women, and no one much cared about your past. He had already traveled west to escape Silver City, now he'd have to travel back east through Silver City to get to the Pecos Valley. At least he knew people around Silver City. He planned to rest before traveling through the desert of *Jornada Del Muerto* (Journey of Death, and later, the White Sands Missile Range). He had never traveled through a desert before, but he figured that there would be fewer Indians there. At the age of seventeen, the kid still had a lot to learn about the Apache.

> Olinger ran out of the saloon and crossed the street as old man Geiss, the cook, crossed the yard of the courthouse and appeared at the front gate. "Olinger," he said stopping the deputy in his tracks, "the Kid has killed Bell." At the same instant the Kid's voice was heard above: "Hello, Bob," said he.
> "Yes," Olinger coolly replied to Geiss as he stared down the barrels of his own shotgun, "and he's killed me too."[11]

My phone rings. The answering machine kicks in.

"Hello... Hello... Hello...?"

Helios rises. His bright eyes reach out over the rows of dark cavernous buildings that make up the Bronx. I could try to sleep or go to the lobby, fetch the mail left uncollected for days, maybe even go out for milk. It's been a long time since I had fresh milk. I should make up a list and do a real shop. Yet something compels me to turn out the lights and sit here as daylight slowly fills the room. Sunstreams highlight the dust swirling through each beam like newspapers in the wind. Called Mormon rain, it accumulates into devil's snow on the floor. Drifts form and fill corners, hide beneath the bed and behind the dresser, cling to fallen socks and misplaced paper clips. How can there be so much movement in the air while I sit so still? From where does such charged energy come? What gives the air such life?

I draw the curtains closed, don my slumber mask, insert earplugs, and do battle with sleep.

Chapter Three

"My name is Anthony Conner, but people call me Tony. I grew up in Silver City, New Mexico with Billy, or Henry as we knew him. More'n two years after Henry busted out of the Silver City Jail, he rode into my brother's ranch...my brother's name is Richard Knight...same mother...older. Do you want to hear about me, or what I know about Billy the Kid?

"As I was saying, Henry rode into the ranch a few years after he escaped up the chimney of...The ranch? Our ranch is located in the Little Burro Mountains forty miles southwest of Silver City. Now are you going to keep interrupting me or let me tell my story?"[12]

The dream continues...

Again, my bodiless soul hovers above the campfire. Below, the strange manchild stands before my sleeping figure, lying there so still and vulnerable. As his darkened figure shadows over my old body, the relief of being released from such a weighty anchor is somewhat diminished by a sudden sympathy for the lifeless hulk below and an inexplicable desire to return to its painful yet defining restraints.

The campfire flames flicker behind his sinister silhouette framed by a large sombrero. The front of his poncho, pulled over his left shoulder, reveals his rifle, barrel low. From above, the sombrero hides his features, but then, as if on cue, my perspective changes. I'm lying on the ground. I feel my body again: my soul nestled in warm flesh, skin itchy beneath a rough wool blanket, face flushed by the flickering fire, and both eyes staring up into the barrel of a Winchester carbine.

"He told my brother what he'd done. Remained about two weeks, but fearing the officers from Arizona might show up any time, he left and never returned."[13]

I feel numb. I'm awake yet immobile as if my body still sleeps. I strain to move, but an invisible rope seems to tighten the more I struggle until it becomes difficult to breathe. I stop struggling and slowly regain my breath.

"Henry was kind of quiet when we was schoolboys, but he took a liking to our teacher, Miss Richards. Henry used to help her around the schoolhouse...oh, chores and stuff. We used to tease him that he was the teacher's pet. Henry didn't like that. After his mama died, he came over to live with us. He worked in my brother's butcher shop in town and I know for a fact that he never stole anything. We left Henry there alone all the time and never noticed anything missing. We couldn't say that about others that had worked there.

"He never swore or acted bad like other kids. When a few of us boys got together and started a minstrel troupe, Billy was head man in the show. Got a standing ovation over at Morrill's Opera House."[14]

Looking up to the silhouette before me, I try to distinguish his features more distinctly. The face beneath the hat is boyish, an obvious stranger to the blade. Dirty blond hair frames bright blue eyes. The most outstanding feature, however, is a pair of bucked teeth, slightly crooked. Otherwise, his eyes betray more charm than gruff as if at any moment he'd break out into a smile that would make one proud to call him a friend.

"A real good singer and dancer, Henry was, but he was smart too. Henry got to be a reader. He would scarce have the dishes washed until he'd be off somewhere reading a book...

Dime novels and such, the Police Gazette. Oh yeah, there was this series about a team of lawmen, vigilantes, who rode the West in search of bad men. What did they call themselves? I remember, 'The Regulators.' Henry loved reading about The Regulators. He wanted to start a gang and call it that, but nobody wanted to join a gang of do-gooders. We all wanted to be badmen."[15]

But with the rifle slung low, he isn't smiling now...

"When Sarah told him he could pick any horse...Sarah Ann Knight, my brother's wife...any horse he wanted out of the corral, he picked the scrubbiest of the lot. Before he left, he told me he was thinking about drifting over to Lincoln County and joining the war. When my brother Richie asked him what side he was going to join, Henry said he did not know."[16]

Chapter Four

"Hello... Hello... Hello...?"

The daily news records time in such a way that gives detail to man's existence, and thus, provides much of the material from which future generations will determine our historic definition. Without the news, how could one ascertain one's own place in time? Therefore, my evening always begins with the newspaper. News stimulates the waking mind, puts one into the mix so to speak. Although my day begins with night, reading the paper is one of the few rituals I share with the waking world. Going outside directly afterwards, however, is another matter entirely.

DRUNK DRIVER DRAGS
TODDLER 20 BLOCKS
License Suspended 64 Times

The Igbo tribe of West Africa, most notably southern Nigeria, believed that the first person with whom you exchange greetings on any given day is the most important. If they are friendly and trustworthy, your day will go well. If they are hostile or indifferent, your day will go badly. Subsequently, it is especially important to ignore everyone until you can exchange greetings with the right person. I believe this to be a wise policy and have found it substantiated many times.

FAMILY OF FIVE
MUGGED AND SHOT ON SUBWAY
Trainload of Commuters Watch Silently

Unfortunately, the times we live in are especially foul

and disagreeable. The newspaper awaits me each evening, perched recklessly behind the front door, waiting to fall into my foyer and release the ugly world into my safe haven. Although I faithfully read it, front to back, even if it takes all night, I find within it enough evil (nation upon nation, government upon citizen, parent upon child) to last indefinitely.

SERBIANS KILL MUSLIMS
MUSLIMS KILL CROATS
CROATS KILL SERBS
Just Another Day in Bosnia

Modern society has returned man to the primeval forest. Meaningless jobs reduce us to operating with our most base instincts. We're like leopards hunting in concrete jungles overgrown with greed: survival of the fittest with money replacing food. Families separate as soon as possible. Parents can't wait for their kids to grow up, get out and support themselves. Upon growing up, children can't wait to commit their parents to nursing homes.

SNIPER KILLS MOM

Modern leadership has reduced itself to governing populations by statistics. The individual feels like a number on a list or a worker ant in an overgrown anthill. Neighborhoods have disintegrated into high-security skyscrapers where apartment dwellers know little of the people next door, or into ghettos where parents keep children indoors for fear of random gunfire.

Such isolation breeds anonymity, and anonymity breeds detachment from all obligation or decency. Words such as "good" and "bad" no longer have a clear definition beyond whether or not one gets caught. How can anyone get caught if everyone is too cynical, hardened, or plain scared to bother paying attention to anything but the most outrageous acts? Print a story about a 5 year old girl tortured to death by her parents and they line up for blocks to view the corpse, tears washing away the guilt of their own crimes against humanity. However, if they hear yelling, smacking, and crying next door, they bury their heads deeper into the pillow, roll over, and try to get some sleep.

NOTEBOOK, PAPER, PEN, AND A
9 MILLIMETER SEMI-AUTOMATIC
Junior Is Ready For Another Day At School

Anonymity breeds lawlessness. No one understands this better than children. Leave a group of children unsupervised in a room, come back in a few hours, and you'll witness a pecking order independent of morality if not complete disorder. Children need parental supervision. Grown-ups either need a strong community consensus of those they know and respect or, if all else fails, the fear of God. Now that man has isolated himself from his fellows, and God for all practical purposes is dead, who will check man's natural inclination towards selfishness in the name of survival of the fittest? In the ensuing chaos, man's Darwinian instinct for self preservation will kick in. He'll justify all kinds of law and order legislation based on "an eye for an eye" mentality of revenge.

Bring back the death penalty, the more painful the better.
It merely reinforces that might is right.
Why waste time, money and energy on rehabilitation,
when corporal punishment is quicker, cheaper and easier?

For every dollar we take away from education, ten is spent on institutionalization. For every new prison we build, another school deteriorates into a holding cell. The kid you toss out on to the street today without skills or self-esteem is the punk that will mug you tomorrow. It's no wonder that youth crime is rising and will continue to rise in spite of all the feeble attempts by politicians, bureaucrats, and the other institutional icons of modern man to stem the tide. The young intuitively develop the very skills they need to survive. What models of behavior are left that offer them a practical alternative?

The Igbo had a simple saying for this, "It takes a village to raise a child."

IS THE KING OF POP
A QUEEN OF PERVERSION?
Boy's Family Charges Singer With Molestation

As the mind of man gets simple, society deteriorates and everyone becomes a potential threat. We've become a nation of falsehoods, a society of strangers, people hiding their true feelings in fear that it *can* and *will* be used against them. The modern forest is more sophisticated, the pecking order more complex, and the armaments more deadly. Without guile, a simple man like myself is unarmed against such weaponry and unprotected from the evils slyly hidden behind the smiling masks worn by others.

WACO WACKOS BURN
Botched Raid on Branch
Davidians Fueled by Fate

Consequently, during my first foray of the day, I'm unable to acknowledge the neighbors. In a co-op, this is not always the best policy. My monthly maintenance bill is automatically paid from my trust account each month. My apartment was paid for in full after *the family tragedy*. Regardless, the co-op board has been trying to rid the building of me since I came of age and has engaged in an endless running battle with my lawyers (praise the Gods I inherited them as well). I'm regarded as an unsuitable tenant, me, who humbly keeps to himself. Where they got this idea, I do not know, but I can hardly exchange greetings with such people. It would be opening the door to their evil without defense.

TEENS TOSS OBJECTS
OFF PARKWAY OVERPASS
Bowling Ball Bashes Baby's Brains 17

Although I've lived here throughout childhood, I know few by name. How can I take a chance greeting strangers?

Any Igbo worth his salt would have eagerly concurred. It was strongly recommended that if one is forced to exchange pleasantries with a hostile presence, one must return home at once and not go out until the next sunrise or risk imminent danger.

However, I can avoid the hostiles that surround me if I make it to the lobby, a bastion of safety. There, doormen patrol around the clock. Doormen are excellent people with whom to exchange first greetings. They always smile and say hello in an unthreatening and sincere manner.

> Driven south, young Henry made his way into Mesilla, just 25 miles north of the border. It was the closest he'd ever been to Mexico, but he might as well have been south of the border for he had never seen so many Mexicans before in all his life. The men wore wide-brimmed hats and loose clothing that seemed very practical to a boy who had just ridden almost 150 miles through some of the roughest country in the southwest. The women made an even deeper impression on the young man. Long black hair, rich auburn skin, and deep dark eyes with an intriguing mixture of sadness and mystery beckoning him, as if the man who possessed the right key to their hearts could unlock the secret to life.
>
> It was here that young Henry started picking up his first phrases of Spanish, a language he took to quite naturally.[18]

I've even learned salutations in the Spanish language as a sign of mutual respect. The doormen respond benevolently, tolerating questions on the subtle differences between *hasta luego* and *hasta la vista* with infinite patience.

> It was also in Mesilla that Henry met another Irish youth his age, Tom O'Keefe, and together they decided to set off for the cattle-rich Pecos Valley in search of work. When asked for his name, Henry answered, "William Antrim, but you can call me Billy."[19]

Such exchanges, always friendly, set a favorable tone, forming a protective armor of positively-charged ions shielding me from the ugly, unsterile world.

> Tom had good news for Billy. If he would meet him just before the sun rose on the outskirts of town where the road forks off to the old Spanish graveyard, Tom would show up later with a pair of horses, one for Billy to ride. Billy was not about to look a gift horse in the mouth and readily accepted. He'd been walking so long he'd taken to plugging the holes in his shoes with newspaper.[20]

Besides affording me the opportunity to go outside with the proper aura of protection required by the Igbo, my *compadres* do many other kind things for their *amigo gringo*. They also sign for the materials I've ordered concerning Billy the Kid and the Old Southwest. Such books and videos are usually delivered door to door by UPS men and the like, but I can't trust interaction with such strangers. As a result, my packages arrive doubly blessed, as long as I can make it to the lobby.

> There was a road, north, through the San Agustin Pass that would take them up through Tularosa and to the U.S. Indian Agency. There, they could get an escort through the Mescalero Apache Indian Reservation and head through a small town called Lincoln, also the county seat for the Pecos Valley. Billy heard it was the best place to inquire about work, especially for men good with a gun. Tom, however, knew a better route east through the Guadalupe Mountains that would take them into the southern tip of Chisum country near the Texas border where there were lots of paying jobs either working for the New Mexican cattle king or against him. Unknown to Billy, the Guadalupe Mountains were located at the southwestern tip of the Indian Reservation and roving bands of renegade Apaches were known to supplement their meager reservation rations with frequent ambushes along the old Indian trails.[21]

A safe time to leave the apartment is shortly after 10 a.m. before I go to bed. By then all the ants have crawled out to work and I can safely leave my den. Maids and maintenance crews, often relatives of the doormen, patrol our dim hallways, but they are friendly. It's best when one addresses them first—*¡Buenos días! ¡Buenas tardes! ¿Una Noches Bonito, no?*

After over a hundred miles of hard riding, out of food and water, they started climbing an old Indian trail over the Guadalupe Mountains. Spying a pool of water at the bottom of a canyon below them, Billy dismounted and took their only canteen down the cliff to fill it up. While at the bottom he heard gunshots echoing through the canyon. He scrambled up the cliff, but by the time he made it to the top, it was too late. There was no sign of O'Keefe, the horses, or anything, including his bedroll. On foot yet again, Billy stumbled down the mountains as the sun set coldly behind him.[22]

The crucial consideration, however, is timing. One mustn't go out during high risk periods of potentially negative encounters. Such times are during morning and evening rush hour. There are also pockets of danger zones during the day. For example: dinner-time delivery boys emanate especially evil ions.

He hid during the day and walked at night. With the mountains descending into arid foothills, the kid grew tired and hungry. Losing the strength to even carry an empty canteen, he threw it away. It was on the third day, no longer caring about the threat of Indians or the heat, that he lay down to rest without realizing he was only a few hundred feet from the Rocky Arroyo river. He lay there in a semi-conscious state unable to move as the sun reached its apex and temperatures soared to 110. Fortunately for the kid, however, a few of Ma'am Jones' ten children had snuck away to play by the river. They overheard the kid moaning and ran to tell their mother.[23]

Timing is everything.

Chapter Five

"If you want to hear about the Kid well then I will tell you. When we found him, it looked like he sorted bobcats for a living. After we dragged him inside, I sat him down at the table. When I took off his boots, he moaned like a panther in heat, and I could see his feet were bleeding and swollen. They struck me as rather small like a woman's and he wore no socks. I offered to wash his feet and put on water to boil. Although it was a warm day, he shivered like a frozen pup, so I wrapped a blanket around his shoulders. I asked when he had eaten last and he said that he had not had any food in three days so I heated him some milk. I will never forget the look of that strange boy sitting at my table hunched over in a blanket with his feet soaking in hot water, his sunburnt face peeling, and his dirty blond hair standing on end like an angry porcupine.

"Still, he did not look no older than my third son, Bill, who at that time was fourteen years old though most said he was big for his age."[24]

I relax completely and the unseen force softens its grip. With each attempt to free myself from its grasp, it retightens its hold in kind, so I lay perfectly still. The world within the circle of light emanating from the campfire begins to swirl wildly like the whirlwind in Dante's second circle of hell. Trees sway at the border as if struggling to hold back the darkness. Leaves spin about the burning logs. Bugs play cat and mouse with flames as sparks leap at the night sky becoming one with the stars above. Grinning, the strange bucktoothed manchild hovers over me.

"When I held out the cup of warm milk for him he said, 'I don't like milk.'
" 'Drink it,' I said. 'You can have some food later. You will not be fit for eating until you rest a little.' But he turned away, so I said, 'Do you want me to hold your nose and pour it down your throat?' When he took the cup, he made a sour face, but when he started drinking, he drank too quickly so I took the cup away and told him just to sip it. When I told him that I was going to put him to bed he said, 'I can sleep right here.' I told him he was worn out and would sleep better in bed. After I helped him to bed, he let me tuck him in.
"He slept all that afternoon and through the night."[25]

He removes his poncho and uses it to wrap the rifle before laying it down beside an empty bed roll, unslept in, as if waiting for an occupant. A large pistol rides his hip, holstered to a thick leather belt. A smaller handgun hangs upside down from his neck noosed around the trigger guard. He looks down as if considering whether to wake me. Carefully, he reaches out for my face like a mother feeling for a temperature, but instead of resting his hand on my forehead, he places it over my mouth. With his other hand he holds my nose, making it impossible for me to draw oxygen. Trying to fight, my muscles freeze. As I frantically strain to move, my body begins to vibrate uncontrollably. The harder I fight, the more I reverberate. If I could just move one muscle, a foot, a finger, I could break the spell, reaffirm contact with the physical world, awake from this nightmare of immobility. My heart beats at my chest trying to leap out and suck in air.

"The next day he introduced himself as Billy Bonney. It was the first time that I had ever heard a last name of Bonney and it sounded made up, but we did not ask such questions west of the Pecos. A man's name was his own business. It was what you did that counted.

"Years later, after Bob Olinger murdered my son John, it was Billy who made Pa keep his promise to me that he would never duel. He also told my son Jim to let him take care of Olinger because my boys were not mixed up in anything and he did not want them to be dragged into the feud. I told Billy that I did not want any of my boys to go after Olinger, and that included Billy. I told him to go away before it was too late, that he was young enough to start a new life somewhere else. 'It's already too late,' he replied.

"When those three killers (Olinger, John Kinney, and Billy Mathews) were assigned to guard Billy on the trip from Sante Fe after his sentencing, I never thought that he would make it back to Lincoln alive."[26]

The safest place for a murderer is to get a job as a deputy.[27]

"When they told me about Billy's escape from the Lincoln County Courthouse, I prayed for J.W. Bell's soul, but thanked the Lord for having spared my husband and sons, for whether they killed Olinger or Olinger them, their souls would have been the devil's bargain. If anyone prayed for Olinger, I cannot tell. His own mother, who I know from church, admitted that he was a sinner and murderer of men and had prayed the Lord's forgiveness for having bore him into the world.

"When I heard that Pat Garrett had shot poor Billy as he backed into Pete Maxwell's room, I prayed for Billy's soul, but I did not pray for Pat. When I heard that Pat was shot in the back years later, I knew it was the Lord's doing: As ye hath sinned, so shall ye be punished."

- Barbara "Ma'am" Jones[28]

Lightheaded, darkness overwhelms me, growing blacker and blacker, until, unable to struggle anymore, I give in and completely relax to my fate. My unbreathing self melts into the ground and becomes one with the absolute stillness and absence of light, feeling, thought. Then, as suddenly as it began, I'm released and find myself gulping for air, heart pounding, skin cold with sweat, throat too dry to swallow, sucking in air thick with devil's snow and swirls of Mormon rain, alone, more alone than I could ever imagine feeling before. Then I hear a voice from outside, in the blind distance, coming closer, an aged, pained voice cracking with loneliness and confusion, seeking me, beckoning for me to answer:

"Hello...?"

Chapter Six

The first day of spring. Dull roots, stirred by vernal rains, shake off winter's icy grip. The air thickens with the smell of last autumn's leaves rotting in the muddy thaw. A sudden humid warmth unearths lost memories of youth as well as the decomposed debris of human refuse heaped winterlong beneath the frozen crust. Springtime sewers overflow, clogged with months of unswept garbage. Suicides and murder victims rise to the slimy surface of the East River. All the foul smells, once hidden by winter's odorless frost, now mingle uncomfortably with the scent of lilacs as they reach for the heavens between discarded prophylactics and soiled under-garments. Like lemon-scented ammonia in public toilets, the fragrance of fresh flowers only seduces you into letting your defenses down. All kinds of fearsome bacteria and toxicants flood unfiltered into the overloaded nervous system.

> *There's guns across the water aimin' at ya,*
> *Lawman on your trail he'd like to catch ya,*
> *Bounty hunters too they'd like to get ya,*
> *Billy they don't like you to be so free.*[29]

When out among the sullied sublunary world, even for a few moments, I can't wait to return homeward to safety, to the pleasure of scrubbing hands clean whether I was exposed to a soiled coin, a public bannister or just the tainted wind. A foulness breeds freely beneath every surface, on the sweaty palms that reach out to shake your hand, behind every grimy door, every false face masking wickedness and hypocrisy. All hide ugly truths, darkened and diluted beyond recognition.

> *Billy don't you turn your back on me.*[30]

The ugly truth is always hidden.

> *Billy don't it make you feel so low down,*
> *To be hunted by the man who was your friend.*
>
> - Bob Dylan[31]

Take Billy the Kid: the more one researches, the more one uncovers.

As history books and dime store novels alike tell it, Henry Michael McCarty, alias Billy the Kid, was shot by Sheriff Pat Garrett in Pete Maxwell's bedroom at Fort Sumner, July 14, 1881.

Beyond this widely accepted fact, however, few are in agreement. To land-grabbing cattle barons, like John Chisum, Billy was both a cattle rustler and a rake who was after both his cows and his beautiful niece, Sallie. To presidential hopefuls like Governor Lew Wallace, author of <u>Ben Hur,</u> William H. Bonney was a thorn in the side of his political ambition. To power-hungry thugs like L.G. Murphy and Jimmy Dolan, the Kid stood in the way of their monopoly over the citizens of Lincoln County. Yet to the Mexican people, uprooted from the land of their forefathers (a land they had so painstakenly wrestled from the Mescalero Apache), El Chivato (the billy goat) was a modern day Robin Hood who stole cows from rich cattle barons (greedy gringos) and generously shared his wealth with the little people (and his seed with the señoritas).

However, to the American public at large (including Washington), fueled by serials like 'The Forty Thieves' (which represented Billy as a cold-blooded killer and leader of a ruthless gang), the kid was a threat to civilized society. The 'Boy Bandit King' was an untamed beast. After all, those who conduct themselves above the law undermine an American dream founded upon the principles that hard work is rewarded and evil punished all for the good of the community, God, and the nation as a whole. In other words, the individual must earn it fair and square. Is that not democracy?[32]

I rode a trail through my neighbor's back yard,
Shooting the bad guys through my handle bars.
Known for my bravery both far and near,
Being late for supper was my only fear.[33]

Yet, what law determines who the most deserving individual is? Natural law? Who, more often than not, reaps the rewards of American democracy: crooks, politicians, the not-so-idle rich? Certainly not the meek. Are not the most worthy often left forgotten, rotting away in dark apartments, knowing too much for their own good, unable to fit into a world of befouled values and morals askewed?[34]

These days I don't know whose side to be on.
There's such a thin line between right and wrong.
I live and learn, do the best I can.
There's only so much you can do as a man.[35]

I know I must go out there sooner or later. Provisions are low and I should mount an expedition for supplies, but the timing must be right. Helios is on the rise again after a long night in hiding. I look out the window and watch as the rose fingers of dawn climb the building across the way. With each new window enveloped by sunlight, reflected rays pierce through me, yet I can't pull my eyes away. Behind each pane, faceless shades ready themselves for day. They'll be rushing to work soon. Hostile and indifferent spirits will fill the fetid air, waiting to piggyback on the unsuspecting soul.

The sun rises. Lemmings flood the streets. Too late to go out there. Time for bed.

I miss Billy the Kid,
The times that he had, the life that he lived.
I guess he must of got caught,
His innocence lost, I wonder where he is.
I miss Billy the Kid.
                    - Billy Dean[36]

Yes, bed.

Floating beneath the stars on a cloudless night, my weightless spirit glides above a dark green forest touched lightly by the moon . . .

Chapter Seven

"Hello . . . ?"

I'm awoken at 5:30 p.m., well before sunset, with a headache among other ills. My eyes hurt from too much dreaming and, while asleep, I somehow sprained an ankle. I sit up, crack neck and back, and draw the curtains open to watch the sun set violet. The streets empty, then fill with lamplight. A few stragglers drag themselves home late to dinners kept warm in the oven. I make out a stick lady struggling, two-fisted, with a puppy on a leash. She snaps the pup's head back as it noses a passing stranger.

When darkness descends and dinners are served, it's late enough to venture outside free of identification, late enough to be free of prying commuter eyes, eyes that rise briefly with disdain to gaze upon the unchained, like myself, as the wretched slaves slouch homeward after a day of pointless labor.

> The Lincoln County, New Mexico, that Billy the
> Kid entered in 1877, was a violent and lawless land.[37]

I dress over my pajamas and stretch on a belt. A baseball cap organizes my hair. Last, but not least, I don a pair of latex examination gloves. I squeeze out of my room into the foyer. Before opening the door, I brace for the smell of the dim, depersonalized hallway. Yes, they vacuum the rug twice a week, but it smells so . . . peopled. I stand before the door, gloved hand upon the knob. My heart beats. I feel dizzy. I take a deep breath and swing open the gate.

My worst fears are immediately realized. I try to move back, but my weighty momentum has shifted me too far forward. I right myself, but it's too late. The door shuts loudly behind me. Standing by the elevator, she peers over, and narrows her eyes.

> Regardless of the crime (murder, theft, bodily disfigurement), few offenders ever suffered punishment in Lincoln. It wasn't until 1877 that anyone bothered to build a jail of sorts. A hole in the ground was dug and covered with a tarp. This served as the only stockade in all of Lincoln County, an area which encompassed almost half of New Mexico.[38]

"Walter," she confirms.

"Mrs. Moss." I pocket my gloved hands. She eyes me suspiciously. "How are you today?" I ask.

"As fine as could be expected," she sighs with a pained look that quickly changes to impatience. "Are you going down?"

"Yes."

"Well then hurry over, the elevator's here."

> One local ruffian, convicted of murder and subsequently pardoned, was defended with these words, "You never saw a better fellow than Ham anywhere; he gets mad quick, and shoots quick, but he's a good shot and never cripples. I really think he is sorry for it afterward when he cools off."[39]

We descend slowly. I hover near the elevator door. She wears a perfume that reminds me of my maternal grandmother when I went to visit her at the Saint Antony Home for the Aged. I remember her distinctly emphasizing that the home was named for Saint Antony of Padua and not Saint Antony the Abbot. Antony of Padua is the patron saint of the poor. Antony the Abbot is the patron saint of grave diggers.

Retirement homes and hospitals have always scared me, especially the florid emanations—like a mix of cheap air freshener and roach balm. What I fear most, of course, is what such malodors mask: death and disease, microscopic bacteria squirming aloft among the dust waiting to be breathed into some fertile host. One mere particle would have a field day in my abundant anatomy. My grandmother began as a nurse at Saint Antony and ended up as a patient. The widow Moss reeks of the same deadly redolence. Within the ugly confines of the elevator, I breath slowly through the mouth.

But Billy had worse dangers to fear in Lincoln than short-tempered pistoleers. The Lincoln County War he so eagerly hurried to join was about to explode into one of the bloodiest range wars in the history of the Southwest.[40]

"Just getting up?" She asked.

"Oh no, got up with the sun, like every morning. Been working at home all day."

"You look tired. Where are you off to this evening?"

"Now? Well . . ." I pull out a hand to scratch my head but quickly return it. "I'm taking a course at Metro College. I just signed up." She eyes the surgical glove.

"Oh yeah, and what course is that?"

"The course? It's a History course, Mythology of the American Southwest, graduate school. They may let me teach soon."

"They would."

"I'm thinking of becoming a professor."

"You don't say. I wonder what your parents would have said to that?"

I stand by the door like a dog with a full bladder.

On the road into Lincoln, Billy, now armed with an antiquated .36 caliber Colt Navy, met up with the outlaw Jesse Evans, who had just signed up as a mercenary for the Murphy/Dolan gang. Billy gave his name as William H. Bonney. It was the first known usage of the formal alias he would keep for the rest of his short life. Evans said they could always use another gun, although he doubted the accuracy of Billy's old percussion pistol.

"You don't want to test it," responded Billy.

Jesse explained that they were set on killing one

John H. Tunstall an Englishman who had settled in the valley. The outsider had set himself up in direct competition with Murphy and Dolan, also known as 'The House' (so-called for the court-like structure built in Lincoln, the largest building in the one-street town, and from which they ruled the region). Billy said he needed to meet a man before killing him. It was bad luck to kill a stranger. Little did the Kid know that the strange Englishman would soon become the father that this poor orphan lad never had.[41]

"I remember your parents. They were such wonderful people, your father and mother, not like couples today always screaming and yelling and blaming each other for what they don't have. The co-op could use more people like your parents. It's a shame what happened. Think how things might have turned out had they not . . ."

The door opens.

"Aren't you getting out?"

I step back. "Oh no, you go. Got to go back up. Forgot my books, silly me. But have a good day Mrs. Moss."

"A good evening, Walter, it's after six. Some of us get out during the day."

Even with John Chisum established as the cattle king of the valley, there was still opportunity west of the Pecos. One such opportunist, Major Lawrence G. Murphy, rested out the Civil War at Fort Stanton, a frontier outpost, while feasting his eyes on the small town of Lincoln nine miles east. As the county seat, he envisioned Lincoln as his base for controlling half of New Mexico. As soon as the war ended, he left the military, but used his connections to enter into a lucrative business of selling beef to an army that was now free to turn its attentions toward ridding the Southwest of the pesky Apache. Instead of building his own ranch and going into direct competition with the well-stocked Chisum, Murphy came up with a novel way of acquiring the extensive numbers of cattle needed to fulfill his contracts to the U.S. Army. After the Civil War ended, thousands of ex-soldiers migrated West in search of employment. Well armed, without direction, and often starving, the ex-major recruited them for a new war, one far less dangerous and far more profitable. They already knew how to fight, but Murphy did need to train them for a new skill: cattle rustling.[42]

Entering the friendly confines of my dark apartment, I peel the gloves off, deposit them in the waste bin, and make my way through the crowded blackness to my room. The answering machine blinks its red beacon. No need to check the message. I know who it is.

Soon Murphy's military contracts expanded to flour, corn and other staples including lucrative (and dubious) arrangements with the Mescalero Apache Indian Agency. He over-counted Indians, falsified vouchers, and inflated beef weights. He left the Indians with little and the government paying a lot. The local civilians in Lincoln didn't fare much better. Murphy soon had a monopoly on all goods coming in and out of the area. At "The Store" local farmers and ranchers purchased goods on credit. Backed by "The Law" (and hired guns if need be), Murphy foreclosed on their farms and ranches when they were unable to pay his exorbitant borrowing rates. If that wasn't enough, he opened "The Bank" and tempted locals to borrow relatively small amounts of money against all their equity. With the younger, but no less ruthless, Jimmy Dolan, Murphy's protege and partner, "The House" dominated the economics and politics of the region.
This is the world into which one naive but well-intentioned Englishman rode with plans to set up shop, all in the name of healthy competition.

His name was John H. Tunstall, and he viewed America as most immigrants of the day: a land of opportunity, where hard work and fair play were rewarded and the corruptions of the old world were left far behind.[43]

The flashing red light leads me to my bed. I press the cancel button and erase it. I'm suddenly tired.

> "Billy lived with me for a while soon after he came to Lincoln County in the fall of 1877. Just before he went to work for Tunstall on the Rio Feliz. No, he didn't work for me. Just lived with me and my cousin George riding the chuck line. He didn't have nowhere else to stay just then.
> "It was at Dick Brewer's ranch, just before Murphy's bank foreclosed on it, that I first met the Kid. Billy had just been turned down for work by Chisum. He had an old pistol in his belt and rode a horse that Pap Jones lent him when he first come into the territory. It was later that Dick introduced Billy to Tunstall. When Tunstall hired Billy he made him a present of a good horse, a nice saddle, and a new gun, a Winchester carbine. My, but the boy was proud. Said it was the first time in his life he ever had anything given him. He said he could not wait to return the old horse to Pap Jones."
> — Frank B. Coe[44]

I unplug the phone, don the slumber mask, and insert ear plugs. I wrestle with sleep until dawn's red fingernails reach through the curtains to scratch my back.

Chapter Eight

To date, Henry Michael McCarty, alias "Billy the Kid," has been the subject of 263 articles and newspaper accounts, 153 books of fiction and nonfiction, 149 copyrighted toy products, 58 moving pictures, 36 government documents (three classified as "Top Secret"), 24 scholarly essays, 14 recorded songs and ballads, six museums, three grave sites, two newsletters, a symphony and a ballet.[45]

In total darkness, I feel my way to the kitchen gliding a finger along the wall and search for breakfast by the refrigerator light. Supplies are dangerously low. I'm forced to mix *Hershey's Instant Hot Chocolate* powder with water and pour it over the last crumbs of *Cocoa Puffs* cereal. Water is added to apricot jelly for juice. An expedition must be mounted and provisions procured or I risk starvation.

However, more people have come to know of Billy the Kid through the movies than any other medium. It is for this reason that, for better or worse, film has had more to do with the mythology of Billy the Kid than any other factor. In so doing, Billy the Kid on film reveals how America views not only the history of the West, but the very mythology of what it means to be an American.[46]

Closing the refrigerator door, I'm embraced once again by the night. Hands occupied, I toe my way down the hallway, negotiating the crowded darkness. I pass sideways between overstuffed bookshelves, step over piles of old newspapers, and squeeze through a door that no longer opens all the way.

This is important, for in America, where few can trace their actual history back beyond a few generations, mythology often becomes their only sense of identity, and therefore, far more essential to one's sense of self than genealogy.[47]

Taking my mind off breakfast, I review the day's schedule and scratch off each accomplished task

> MON
> 1) ~~Wake~~
> 2) ~~Eat~~
> 3) Shower (wash hair?)
> 4) Dress
> 5) Clip fingernails
> 6) Outside
> a) mail
> b) grocery

Two so far. The next three will be easy. I draw a box around them. I'll return in triumph after they're completed.

> When history is impossible to trace, mythology takes over.[48]

INTERIOR: HOUSE LIBRARY—EVENING FADE IN

The room is fitted in late 18th-19th century English decor: an oriental rug, velvet drapes, flocked wallpaper. Furnishings include a Chippendale sofa of inlaid marquetry, two Louis XIV revival armchairs, and a grand piano. Lined neatly with bound volumes, a long walnut bookcase occupies the back wall.

Two men enter through an archway framed with laced portieres. One man is dressed like an English gentleman smoking a pipe. The other is dressed like an American western outlaw wearing a holster with a pistol.

BILLY THE KID
What kind of room is this?

TUNSTALL
This is the library, Mr. Bonney.

Billy looks about in childlike wonder as Tunstall lights his pipe.

> BILLY THE KID
> You don't see much of rooms like this around these parts. Look at all them books. Have you read all that?

Tunstall smiles and lowers his pipe.

> TUNSTALL
> Many, but not all. Some books are meant for other purposes than reading cover to cover. This set of volumes, for example, is an encyclopedia. You use it for reference... to look up things.

> BILLY THE KID
> Like what?

> TUNSTALL
> For example, earlier today you inquired about my accent and why I carry no sidearms.

> BILLY THE KID
> Yeah, you talk like a King of Diamonds, but act like the King of Clubs.

> TUNSTALL
> I come from England. Our ways are different over there. You could read about England in an encyclopedia.

> BILLY THE KID
> I don't take to far away places. Seems a waste of time thinking about where I ain't. I like to think about where I am.

TUNSTALL
What about your forefathers, do you not
care about the country from whence
they came?

BILLY THE KID
My mother said we holler from a place
called Ireland, but I never gave it much
thought.

TUNSTALL
Are you not interested in learning about
your past?

BILLY THE KID
The past don't concern me. I only care
about today—right here, right now.

TUNSTALL
There are those who might consider that
a practical view.

Billy rests his hand atop his pistol.

BILLY THE KID
Oh I'm practical all right.

Tunstall casually lights his pipe.

TUNSTALL
Your reputation with a pistol precedes
you, Mr. Bonney. Please forgive my forwardness, but may I ask if you also possess the ability to read?

BILLY THE KID
I had me some schooling.

TUNSTALL
Have you ever read the Bible?

BILLY THE KID
Ma read parts to me.

TUNSTALL
Have you read it since then?

BILLY THE KID
Never owned a copy.

TUNSTALL
Do you own *any* books, William?

BILLY THE KID
Books weigh a saddle bag down.

Tunstall reaches to the bookcase, pulls out a Bible and hands it to Billy.

TUNSTALL
Accept this copy as a gift.

Holding the Bible like it was fine china, Billy looks down at the book, hesitates, and looks back up at Tunstall.

BILLY THE KID
I... I can't carry something like this around. Why... it weighs near as much as my six-shooter and I'm not about to lay that down.

TUNSTALL
What if you had a place to lay your Bible, William, or for that matter, anything else that weighed you down?

BILLY THE KID
What do you mean by that?

TUNSTALL
I mean that I am offering you a job, my

dear fellow. You told me before that you found Murphy's methods distasteful. You also said that you would never shoot a man in the back or one that was unarmed, but how long will you be able to say that if you ride for Murphy? Hang your spurs here and you can earn an honest living. Is that not what you really want? Is that not what your dear mother would want?

                    BILLY THE KID
My dear mother's dead, Mr. Tunstall, and I'm wanted, dead or alive, for shooting the man that insulted her.

                    TUNSTALL
You said before that you are not concerned with the past. Well, neither am I. I care about the kind of man you are today, Mr. Bonney, the man standing before me, right here, right now. That's the man I want working for me.

                    BILLY THE KID
But I've never punched cows Mr. Tunstall. I don't even know if it's in me.

                    TUNSTALL
I believe whatever William Bonney decides to do, will be done.

Billy looks back down at the Bible in his hands.

                    TUNSTALL
I'm offering you a way to start over again, man, a way to wipe the slate clean, to begin anew. With the past behind you, your future is an open book.

                         53

BILLY THE KID
I just don't know Mr. Tunstall.

TUNSTALL
Don't make up your mind right away, my
boy, just promise me that you will give it
some thought. In the mean time, you are
welcome to stay the night and leave in
the morning. Darkness has settled upon
us and I fear a storm is brewing.

Tunstall smiles a moment before resuming.

TUNSTALL
It would be a shame for that Bible to get
wet.

FADE OUT[49]

Referring back to the list, I update my progress.

3) ~~Shower~~ (wash hair?)
4) ~~Dress~~
5) ~~Clip fingernails~~

Each achievement, each bold scratch of pen, marks my
daily progress. Already a day well spent, now to forge
ahead.

6) Outside
a) mail
b) grocery

Grocery . . . I should expand upon this. If I'm to go out
there, I should be prepared to face the wilds in as civilized
a manner as possible. Organization is the weapon of choice.
The list needs detail.

b) grocery
- Hershey chocolate bars
- Marshmallow Fluff

- Skippy Honey Nut Peanut Butter
- Reddi-Wip Instant Whipped Cream
- Mini-Oreo Cookies & Cocoa Puffs
- Milk
- Rolaids

I hear what sounds like a puppy yelping, a bark mixed with more fear than intimidation. I didn't know my neighbors owned a dog. Not Mrs. Moss of course. Nothing could live with her I fear, not even a dog. These two are a childless couple. The man has a voice that goes through walls.

"Shut up, you mangy mutt!"

Now they've got something new to fight about.

"Good lord!" His voice rises. "Come over here. Look at this. I thought you said you walked the dog?"

Such interruptions are terribly distracting. How can anyone get any work done? Her voice is so low, I can't make out her response. I grab a glass from the kitchen and cup it against the wall, my ear pressed to the bottom.

"Did I want the dog?" He asks accusingly.

"I thought it was your idea," she answers meekly. I can barely make her out.

"My idea? So now it's my idea. You always say it's my idea when anything goes wrong."

"No I don't."

"Are you calling me a liar?"

"I didn't call you a liar. I just said it wasn't my . . ."

"Now you want to change the subject. We're talking about the dog here, about the mess *your* dog made on that brand new rug, the rug that was bought with *my* money, the money I sweat *my* balls off for and *you* throw away on stupid pets."

"But it was . . ."

"Don't but me," his voice crescendos. "Who's responsible for the dog?"

"I am, but . . ."

Now shouting, "Answer me—don't but me!" There's a pause before he speaks again. This time his voice is ominously low.

"Now, who's responsible for the dog?"

"I am."

"So who's responsible for that shit on the rug?"

"I am."

"Then why did you let it happen?"

"But . . ."

"Don't but me!" I hear the hollow sound of a fist hitting the side of a face. The puppy resumes its frightened barking from the other room. Involuntarily, I spring back losing contact with the glass. I carefully place it upon the wall again.

"Look what you made me do."

I make out muffled sobs.

"When I let you get the damn dog, you said you'd take care of it. Now we've got a little eat, piss, shed and shit machine on our hands. You say you want kids? You can't even take care of a dog. Are you listening to me?!"

"Yes, yes," she says between sobs.

"LOOK AT ME WHEN I'M TALKING TO YOU!"

"I'm sorry, please, I'm looking, I'm looking."

"Train the fucking dog or you get more of *this*!"

I picture his hand raised again. She cringes and covers up.

> In conclusion, the actual facts concerning Billy the Kid, or anyone's life for that matter, has no historical relevance or meaning, per se. One's actual life remains private, unexposed, a mystery. Its meaning, value, or actuality exists only in what people believe to be true. The public mind determines history and, subsequently, its relevance or meaning from that context. This historical consensus then, reveals not only how we view ourselves, but how we wish to be viewed by others. Billy the Kid, as a factual entity, exists only in the present public perception (continually in flux) and therefore functions as just another barometer of the American mind.[50]

A door slams. In the distance, frightened barking resumes. Then I hear the man's voice merge with the puppy's in the echo of the other room, "Damn mutt!"

There's a thud like a foot kicking fur-lined ribs. The puppy whines in short frantic yelps. My phone rings sending a lightning bolt through my heart. The glass drops from my hands and crashes to the floor. The answering machine clicks in. I desperately clasp my hands to my ears. I don't want to hear anything anymore.

CUT TO

EXTERIOR: PORCH—EVENING

Tunstall walks out of his house on to the porch. Lighting a pipe, he looks into the distance deep in thought. Unseen by Tunstall, Billy walks out of the darkness and stands at the bottom of the stairway.

> BILLY THE KID
> Excuse me Mr. Tunstall, are you busy?

Startled out of his deliberations, Tunstall turns to face Billy.

> TUNSTALL
> Oh, good evening William. I'm never too busy for a friendly chat. Is there something troubling you, my son?

As Billy climbs the stairs to the porch, light shines upon the Bible in his hand.

> BILLY THE KID
> I've been looking over this here book you give me. I believe I have a question.

> TUNSTALL
> Tell me, my good man, how have you enjoyed your reading?

BILLY THE KID
Well, it starts out riding high and wide,
gets bogged down a bit in all that beget-
tin', then whips up agin'.

Tunstall smiles benevolently.

TUNSTALL
Where are you up to now?

BILLY THE KID
That's what I wanted to ask you about. It
says in this here *Book of Moses* that
God gave out these commandments.

TUNSTALL
Yes, ten of them.

BILLY THE KID
Got no problem with most of them, at
least them I make sense of, but this one,
this deal about not killing. What do they
mean by that?

TUNSTALL
Ah, "Thou shalt not kill." According to
prevailing Protestant and Orthodox
Christian Practices, that is The Sixth
Commandment.

BILLY THE KID
But a man's got to kill things to survive.

TUNSTALL
Indeed, my dear fellow, but I believe that
God meant one must not kill his fellow
man.

BILLY THE KID
But that just don't make no sense. A

58

man has got to protect his self. Some
people just need killing.

TUNSTALL
Remember when we first met, you
asked why I never wore a gun?

BILLY THE KID
You said you didn't need one.

TUNSTALL
You see, William, violence only begets
more violence. Personally, I would rather
be killed than kill.

BILLY THE KID
Then you're lucky to be alive, Mr. Tunstall.

TUNSTALL
It's not luck, William. It's God's will.

BILLY THE KID
And if someone dusts you front to back?

TUNSTALL
Then that is God's will as well.

BILLY THE KID
Will it be God's will when I dust the man
that dusts you?

TUNSTALL
No, William, you must not dirty your
hands. We all must learn to forgive. God
will punish he that sins.

Billy opens the Bible and points.

BILLY THE KID
But what about this part here. It says...

Billy reads haltingly.

BILLY THE KID
..."And if any mischief follow, then thou
shalt give life for life, eye for an eye,
tooth for tooth."

TUNSTALL
Only the authorities can administer such
laws.

BILLY THE KID
But it says nothing about authorities
here, Mr. Tunstall. And look at the way
the law was run in old Egypt. That don't
seem a far cry from Lincoln County
today. Them Israelites got about as
much justice out of this Pharaoh and the
Egyptians as we can expect from Murphy and the Sante Fe Ring.

TUNSTALL
You have an interesting argument,
William, and I'm impressed with your
diligence, but if you read on, you will find
that God *does* punish the Egyptians and
the Pharaoh. The parallel you draw
between the wanderings of the Israelites
and our situation is acute, but have faith,
William. *Our* Egyptians— Murphy, Dolan
and the Sante Fe Ring—they shall *also*
be punished. You see, my son, civilization is coming to the Southwest. Swords
shall be melted into plowshares. The
desert will blossom into ranches and
farms. Casinos and houses of ill-repute
will be transformed into schools and

churches. Those who don't change with the times are doomed; those who do, will reap the rewards of their conversion. Yes, William, the West is changing and it will be a wonderful thing to behold, a wonderful thing indeed.

As Tunstall finishes his speech, a cowboy rides into the ranch through the main gate, dust billowing behind his speeding horse. As he dismounts, fellow ranch hands surround him and voices rise up in an angry chorus.

> TUNSTALL
> Excuse me, William. Who goes there? Is anything wrong?

The cowboy leads his horse up to the porch followed by the other men and enters into the light. It's Richard Brewer, Tunstall's foreman.

> BREWER
> I'm afraid so, Mr. Tunstall. It's about the cattle, sir, the cattle we had grazing south of the Rio Feliz.

> TUNSTALL
> Speak up, good man.

> BREWER
> Well, they've been stampeded, right through our camp destroying everything. We spotted rustlers heading northeast towards the Murphy ranch. I recognized Jesse Evans and his gang with Morton, Baker and Hill loaded for bear. Those boys have the Murphy/Dolan sign branded to the bone. It doesn't take much head scratching to figure out who's behind this.

TUNSTALL
Anyone injured?

BREWER
One of ours and he ain't breathing.

BILLY THE KID
I bet their fixin' to change those brands
as soon as they get 'em home. I say we
ride over to Murphy's ranch tonight and
wait for them to arrive. Then we can give
them a dose of their own medicine, eye
for an eye, tooth for tooth, *lead for lead.*

A murmur of assent is raised among the men.

TUNSTALL
Now William, men, we do not know for
sure that Murphy and Dolan are behind
this. It would be better for us to collect
evidence, make affidavits and then I can
present this to Governor Axtall in person. I will ride to Sante Fe myself and
demand a new sheriff. Then we can put
the perpetrators on trial.

BILLY THE KID
But what are we gonna do *now*? Aren't
they gettin' away with the real evidence.

TUNSTALL
We must document the full story, and not
take the law into our own hands. Then
when I go before the Governor, he'll be
forced to take action.

BILLY THE KID
But what makes you think Murphy, with
his connections to the Sante Fe Ring,
hasn't already gotten to the Governor?

TUNSTALL

If that is the case, by Axtall's inaction, I will be able to present an even more convincing case to Washington if need be. I have a new partner, Alex McSween. He runs my store in town, but he's also a licensed lawyer. He worked for Murphy and Dolan before me until he refused to do their dirty work. With his assistance, Murphy and Dolan's days are numbered, but we must do it legally. I must have no blood on my hands when I go to meet the governor or travel to Washington. Only from atop the moral high ground can we convince the authorities that the time has come for New Mexico to take its honored place among the rest of the United States of America. The Lord has shown us the light. The time has come for us to lead the way. Abide by my wishes men and welcome a new era to Lincoln, one of law and order and freedom from under the monopolistic yoke of Murphy, Dolan and "The House."

Billy looks down at the Bible in his hands.

BILLY THE KID

Lord, I hope you're right.

FADE OUT[51]

The outside hallway reverberates with tension. Tears, yelps and shouts, long ended, echo off the cheap ribbed paneling, seeping into cavernous elevator shafts and tumbling into the basement below. Can I go out there now and wallow in such ill will? There *are* other things on my list that need doing.

7) Tasks
a) tape "Billy the Kid vs.
 Frankenstein" (ch 5, 2-4pm)
b) organize closet
8) Visit?????

The red light on my answering machine blinks accusingly.

~~8) Visit?????~~

I skip to the next item.

9) Dinner
10) Sunrise
a) make out new schedule
b) bed prep
    - unplug phone
    - draw curtains
    - slumber mask
    - earplugs
11) Bed

It's hopeless. How can I ignore the light?

"He was universally liked. The native citizens loved him because he was always kind and considerate to them and took much pleasure in helping them and providing for their wants. He thought nothing of mounting his horse and riding all night for a doctor or for medicine to relieve the suffering of some sick person."[52]

The phone rings again. I unplug it.

"Billy was a graceful and beautiful dancer, and when in the company of a woman, he was at all times extremely polite and respectful. Also while in the presence of women, he was neat and careful about his personal appearance. He was always a great favorite with the women, and at a dance he was in constant demand; yet with it all, he was entirely free from conceit or vanity. It was just natural for him to be a perfect gentleman."[53]

I don't have the stomach to listen to these messages anymore, nor the heart to erase them. I can delay no longer. I must go out there. For food, yes, but I must also stop him.

"The Kid often said that he loved Mr. Tunstall better than any man he ever knew. I have always believed that if Mr. Tunstall had lived, the Kid, under his guidance, would have become a valuable citizen, for he was a remarkable boy, far above the average young men of those times and he undoubtably had the making of a fine man in him."
Mrs. Susan Barber (McSween)[54]

The answering machine clicks in again. I cut it off.

"Hel..."

I'll go tomorrow.

Chapter Nine

On that fateful winter day of February 18, 1878, the sun rose majestically, unencumbered by wind or cloud. Prairie dogs led their young out of the burrow to play as snakes and panthers took the morning off to nap under the warm eye of heaven. Even golden eagles, perched on their nests, seemed satisfied to quietly survey their dominion; or take an occasional romp in the cool, azure sky, forgetful of the hunt; and for the first time since their maiden glide as grey-feathered innocents, lean over and dive headlong into space, as if reminded again of the sheer joy of flight.

Grasping to his breast the papers concerning L.G. Murphy's illegal activities, John H. Tunstall took a deep, satisfying breath of the dry, crisp New Mexican air. He stepped up to the buckboard of his wagon and turned to address his men. The English gentleman-turned-cattleman surveyed the horizon and remarked that he could think of no finer a day to venture forth on the long journey to Sante Fe for a meeting with the governor. "It seems that God himself hath blessed this noble quest for justice." Before sitting down, he added, "In Sante Fe, I plan to purchase new shirts, jeans, and boots to restock the store in Lincoln. I'll bring back extra pairs of each for every one of my loyal band. If we are to be the new breed of citizen in Lincoln County, we might as well look the part."

The ranch hands waved their hats and cheered, all except Billy the Kid. As soon as his compadres quieted, he stated soberly, "God blessed or no, we ain't lettin' you ride lonesome Mr. Tunstall."

"Now, now, William, men, there's no need for worry," Tunstall replied. "I'm an unarmed man on a simple business trip. An armed escort would only attract attention. That could escalate into violence and violence must be avoided at all costs."

"I hate to say it, but I agree with the Kid, Mr. Tunstall," replied the foreman, Dick Brewer. "These hills are crawling with Murphy men itching to lay you out proper. Riding alone to Sante Fe is like diving into a bear's den smeared with honey."

"But Richard, I have nothing to fear," Tunstall insisted. "As far as Murphy is concerned, I am riding into Sante Fe on a wagon for supplies. Furthermore, God is on our side."

"God may be on our side Mr. Tunstall," said the fearless Billy the Kid, "but he ain't packin' no lead. Like it or not, I'm doggin' you, be it in a pack or alone."

"It seems I cannot fight you," Tunstall consented, "but I must insist that the party be small and act only as a deterrent."

"Of that you can be assured, Mr. Tunstall," said Brewer. "Middleton, Waite, and McCloskey... hey where is McCloskey?"

"Rode out early this morning," John Middleton reported. "Said something about a woman."

"A woman?" said Billy disbelieving. "That yellow-bellied turkey never talked of no woman before."

"Forget it, Kid," replied Brewer. "Widenmann, you go. You're a better shot with a rifle anyway. I got to talk to that McCloskey. For a hand that just joined up, he's doing little to prove himself. Never around when you need him."

"And what about me?" demanded Billy.

"All right, Kid. You could outshoot the devil himself, so you might as well go too." As the Kid started to check his weapons with a flourish, Brewer turned aside to Waite and said in a low voice, "Keep an eye on him Fred. You're about the only soul who can reason him."

Frederick T. Waite, a Choctaw from Indian territory, nodded silently. Although he dressed as a white man to avoid persecution and rarely spoke, he never denied his heritage. As far his compadres were concerned, he carried his weight proper, handy with horse, rope and gun, which was about all they cared about, regardless of race, creed, or color. The Kid always shifted his ears forward when he heard Fred address him as "Little Coyote," but Billy wasn't the only one who listened intently when Fred chose to utter a few well-chosen words.

"Tie an extra horse to the back of the wagon," Brewer added. "At the first sign of trouble, all of you, take to the hills, don't stand and fight. That includes you Billy. I don't want anyone to take any chances with Mr. Tunstall's life. Did you hear that Billy?"

"Yeah, just fine, Dickey-boy," said the Kid loading the chambers of his revolver. "Take no chances." He snapped the cylinder back in place.[55]

Behind my apartment door I stand—gloved hand upon knob, ear upon surface—listening into the hallway for trouble on the other side. No neighbor's door swings open or slams its ugly echo. No screeching children defy parents. No squeaking shopping carts lug *Wonder Bread* and *Shake N' Bake*. I strain to hear surly delivery boys crinkling packages of prescriptions or Chinese food. All quiet. I crack open the door and peek through. Nothing. I bravely lean out and look both ways. All clear. I step out and softly close the door behind me, pressing lightly until the lock clicks in. Now I'm committed.

As I walk towards the elevator, I check over my shoulder. It feels as if there's something waiting to surprise me, as if a hand will reach out at any moment, grab me by the scruff of the neck, and shout, "Hey you! Where do you think you're going?"

Although but a few seconds, the elevator seems to take countless minutes. Desperately, I pray for it to arrive, but fear the doors opening to a crowded cab revealing a horrid mix of foul odors, nudging fingers, and serrated stares. Then I hear it change direction. Its cold mechanics crescendo closer, slow, stop, click.

Behind me, an apartment door suddenly opens.

As they rode along the byway to Sante Fe, the sun warmed each rider's shoulders. Soon, they relaxed their normally erect postures and the pace seemed to slow in spite of the long journey. The horses, sensing their riders' mood, no longer needed steering, but followed the well-beaten trail. The riders, getting lost in their own conversation and the casual air, split up a little. Billy and Middleton faded a few hundred yards to the rear as Brewer and Widenmann rode point in front of Tunstall's wagon. Fred Waite scouted ahead for trouble and reported back once, switching horses with Tunstall's trailer, before setting out again, this time checking the rear.

Near five o'clock, with the winter sun giving off the last warmth of the day, Widenmann spied a flock of turkeys ahead, and being that time for thinking about setting up camp and cooking a hot meal after a long day's ride, he suggested that they bag a few.

"You bonney lads go ahead," replied Tunstall. "I'll stay with the wagon." Before leaving, Widenmann offered Tunstall his rifle, but the noble Englishman refused. "You will need that, good fellow, will you not? Now go on, I can already taste a delicious turkey supper."

"We'll be only a minute, Mr. Tunstall," said Brewer and off they rode. As Brewer and Widenman descended into a gully, Tunstall noticed dust up ahead. It couldn't be Waite, he was behind them. As the dust got closer, he realized it was not one rider, but many, and they were riding fast, but he had difficulty seeing with the sun setting directly behind them. He looked back over his shoulder and noticed that Billy and Middleton had faded far back. He could no longer see Brewer and Widenmann nor be sure where they were. He could now make out at least twenty horsemen silhouetted by the sun. As the riders approached, Tunstall still couldn't recognize any of the men, but he could see one thing clearly, they were riding hard and they were heavily armed.[56]

First, a floppy-eared puppy topples out in the hallway and strains against a leather leash to sniff my toes before looking up. Seeing an enormous towering body attached, he cowers away in fear. The woman, with her back to me as she locks the door, wears a hat so large that it appears to rest upon a headless body. When she turns, my presence startles her. She drops her keys, which in turn startles me. Before she quickly bends to the floor, I notice a recent bruise below her left eye. She rises, head lowered and stands there, pausing it appears, still resolute in her task to walk the dog, yet hesitant about entering any elevator with me. Then I hear the elevator doors closing behind me.

I reach back as fast as I can, bump my elbow, and miss the door. I stick in a foot. The door closes and bites it painfully until I reach in and jiggle the gate's rubber gums. Finally, its jaw relaxes releasing my foot. I hold its mouth open and turn to the woman who is cringing in her doorway, the puppy hiding behind her leg.

"I've got the door."

The riders split up 100 yards in front of Tunstall's wagon. A group of riders headed left toward the gully where Brewer and Widenmann were chasing turkeys. Another group rode right to cut off Billy and Middleton. A third group approached Tunstall. As their long shadows reached the fair Englishman, he finally recognized the five riders: Jesse Evans and gang members William "Buck" Morton, Frank Baker, Tom Hill, and Manuel Segovia, nicknamed "the Indian" although he shared little of such noble blood. Could it be by mere coincidence that they happened to be the very men named by Tunstall's witnesses for cattle rustling and murder the night before? Here was the "lawful posse" Sheriff Brady assembled on Murphy's behalf to arrest Tunstall. Jimmy Dolan followed behind at a safe distance and appeared to shout instructions. Close enough to block the sun completely, the riders, now silhouettes, pulled out their guns.[57]

She short-steps into the elevator cab reeling in the puppy. The puppy glues itself so tightly around her ankles that she stumbles slightly as she hits the lobby button. Wedging herself into the far corner, the puppy hides behind her bony, spinach-veined ankles.

Feeling like Thrasymachus gazing upon the eyes of the dead, I can't resist looking at the woman across from me, her face hidden beneath the brim of her whimsy. She wears stiletto high-heeled shoes which seem highly inappropriate for dog walking. Tight black leotards accentuate mannikin thin legs. She wears an orange paisley vest and a loose white shirt buttoned up to the collar (praise the Gods!) but fails to hide a pair of hands and wrists so bony and fragile the skin seems more like webbing. The momentary glimpse I had of her skullish face betrayed features which once may have been attractive. I catch a glimpse of circular earrings which appear larger than her shrunken ears.

With her gaunt body, she appears to suffer from anorexia, a disease I fail to understand. I'm reminded of a childhood memory, a grainy black and white film clip I once saw as a young boy on the liberation of Aushwitz during World War II. As bulldozers shoveled mounds of the unclothed dead into large graves, the body of a women, teetering on the edge of the ditch, was finally nudged over by a blackened boot. As the camera followed her tumbling sideways over bodies, her dark hair hid her face, her arms flailed like loose string, her lifeless breasts sagged sideways, her pubic hair, black against the palest of white skin. I was filled with dread and experienced a fear so primal, completely beyond explanation, the kind you never outgrow. Later, I experienced nightmares of being dumped over the precipice by a bulldozer with the other bodies.

As the elevator descends, lifting my bodyweight slightly off my feet, I feel a strange chill through my back and shoulders, and I'm transported back in time to that childhood vision, that all-encompassing moment of which only children seem susceptible. Falling among the corpses again, I'm tangled in the dead woman's arms, her hair blinding me, tumbling over the other bodies to the muddy bottom until she lands on top of me and I'm buried alive suffocating in her rotting thatch for all eternity.

The elevator stops. The door opens. All three of us stand immobile.

Sensing some sort of pursuit, the small flock of turkeys scrambled out of the gully with Brewer and Widenmann hot on their tails. At this point, with the fowl fenced in and confused, Brewer and Widenmann could have jumped off their horses and bagged their quarry by hand, but a real cowboy doesn't dismount unless absolutely necessary. Instead, each tried to grab the birds by the neck while mounted. This made for a great challenge and much joviality. The turkeys, not amused at this play, flayed their wings stirring up the dust and gobbled loudly drowning out the men's laughter as the hunters leaned over and grasped handfuls of air. In the confusion, the lead bird found a way out sending them all further down the gully. Brewer and Widenmann could have then taken out their rifles and easily plugged a few, but that did not seem sporting, and although neither of them conversed on the issue, they were in mutual agreement that the way to proceed was to follow the turkeys' lead and continue the pursuit.

At the bottom, the turkeys were again trapped. Brewer reached down and finally grabbed one by the neck. In his glee, he raised the captured fowl above his head and shouted to Widenmann, "Hey Bob, looky here, don't this one paint a nice picture."

That's when they heard the first shots.[58]

They exit the elevator and find unsure footing on the slippery lobby floor. She wobbles gingerly on high heels. The puppy strains against a short leash scurrying in place and flopping on its side. Since we carefully avoided salutations, I feel no Igbo would judge me wrong in proceeding. Still, before following, I check the hallway. At the end, I see the doorman assisting an older woman with her two-wheeled shopping cart up the stairs. She's short, wide, and wearing a thick coat . . .it's Mrs. Moss and she's heading this way! Before they see me, I take cover.

I hear Mrs. Moss's voice cackle, "Hold the elevator, please."

I quickly press the *close door* button, breaking a fingernail which sticks through my glove like a broken bone through skin.

"Hold the elevator. Can't you hear me?"

Protecting my wounded finger, I press myself tightly against the paneling.

"Hold the door! Who's in there?"

Please, *please*, close the door.

"I'm almost there, can't you hold the door just one second?"

At this point, dear reader, you may want to pause before reading further. The following account of the incident between Murphy's blood-thirsty "posse" and the kind-hearted Tunstall may not be suitable for the tender ears of young innocents or women in a family way. Of the countless dastardly deeds recorded during that short epoch of history so aptly named the Wild West, the following ranks as the most dastardly and desperate of them all.

Buck Morton was the first to get within range. As the trusting Englishman raised his right hand in salutation, clearly unarmed, Morton raised his rifle and fired, shooting the unsuspecting gentleman through his tender heart. With one hand grasping his noble breast, the other raised to the heavens, the good squire fell off his modest chariot and onto the ground. As he wallowed in the dust gasping for fresh air, the evil Jesse Evans pulled out his revolver and shot the helpless soul in the back of the head. To make sure the deadly deed was done, Morton dismounted and crushed the dying man's head with the butt of his carbine as Segovia "the Indian" picked up stones and pelted the twitching torso. Baker, not to be outdone, finished the devil's work with two barrels of buckshot nearly cutting the courtly corpse in

73

two. Gleefully, Dolan witnessed the dirty work of his bestial pawns, not missing one tasty detail. Later, he'd relate the morbid merriment to Murphy over drinks and derisive laughter.

The fallen prince's horse, confused at his master's sudden immobility, licked a bloody ear. The outlaw Jesse Evans, untouched by this tender display of loyalty, re-cocked his pistol and gleefully shot the poor beast between the eyes, laughing with a chill that the devil himself found distasteful. Their bloodlust boiled, the blue jean clad gargoyles began mutilating the lifeless body of Tunstall with jagged rocks and an axe from the wagon in such a ghastly and unspeakable fashion that I ask to be forgiven by historians and antiquarians alike for not objectively detailing such deprivations, and failing in my duties as a writer to precisely record history. For those who desire such facts, I pray you find satisfaction elsewhere. Suffice it to say that in capping off their twisted sport, one Frank Baker joined in to help Hill and Morton lay the poor horse besides its kingly master. Using Tunstall's coat and hat as pillows, they fashioned the pair as if sleeping side by side while facing heaven. Their laughter over this final display of divine mockery, echoed ominously over the hills.

Pinned down by Murphy's forces at a distant hillside, Billy blasted away at the enemy with his six-shooter, John Middleton cowering at his feet. As bullets grazed his youthful waves of hair, hot tears streamed down his rose-bloomed cheeks.

Miles away, the real Indian, Fred Waite, turned back from his scouting duties to join the others when he spied a golden eagle flying above him. Such birds were considered by the Choctaw to be sacred. The heavens sent messages of portent through the actions of our flying cousins. One had to watch and listen in order to interpret their actions.

As the great bird's shadow passed overhead, it suddenly swung down in the direction of where Waite had left his compadres. It swept its large wingspan inches above the ground, opened its razor sharp talons, and snatched a prairie dog puppy for dinner.

Waite spurred his horse knowing he was too late.[59]

As I enter the apartment, the phone is ringing. I throw my hands over both ears and hum loudly until it passes.

"Little Coyote," Waite whispered into the grieving Kid's ear, "I think it's time to start that ranch on the Penasco like we planned."[60]

I tend to my wounded finger and revise tomorrow's schedule.

Chapter Ten

According to most historians, western frontier afi-
cionados and other amateurs whose books crowd library
shelves and discount bookstores, John H. Tunstall's death
signifies the official beginning of the Lincoln County War.
However, this supposition can only be true if the definition
of war is written in blood alone. Otherwise, a more modern sensibility marks this violent action as the point where
the escalating conflict made a transition from a "cold" war
to a "hot" one. And hot it undoubtedly became. Of all the
range wars waged during the 30 year period of post-Civil
War southwestern U.S. settlement (commonly known as
the "Wild West"), few were more steeped in blood than
the contest for Lincoln County. Even the notorious Johnson
County War paled in comparison.[61]

Darkness. Silence. Warmth.

Earplugs inserted, I lie in bed buried beneath the covers.
I lie completely still, breathe my own dioxidous air, listen to
my heart beat. The thickness of night blankets my soft
cocoon. Out there, I imagine the world asleep—lights out
but for street lamps, the occasional car, or some unfortunate
soul shaken out of slumber by a bursting bladder, unhappily
forced to enter the harsh light in a cold search for relief.

ACT TWO

*The lights dim, but before the curtain rises an old English
song "The Three Ravens" fades in on guitar and violin.
Played mournfully like a funeral dirge, the singer sings with
much expression.*

Down the hill in yonder green field,
(Down a down, hey down, hey down)
There lies a knight slain under his shield.
(With a down, down, derry, derry, down)

His hounds they lie down at his feet,
(Down a down, hey down, hey down)
So well they do their master's keep.
(With a down, down, derry, derry, down)

The curtain rises.[62]

But me, here, alone in the belly of my bed, breathing slower and slower, heart releasing its grip and growing lighter, beating less and less until a single tap nudges gentle waves through my body like a babbling brook in the garden of serenity. Each pulse, like a pebble tossed in the center of a pond, forms ripples of relaxation flowing happily into unburdened limbs. I feel my soul pass through these fingertips as the ruffled sound of water ebbs through mossy rocks, down hillsides into burgeoning pools, over embankments and into rivers, and finally returning to the all-embracing mother, the sea, embracing her children while singing sweetly a tidal song of peace and harmony with the moon and stars.

Floating away on the curves of her canzonet, her lullaby of space and time, her *Novus Magnificat* into the fifth dimension, leaves me both empty and filled with everything and nothing, a complete sense of personhood yet fully a part of the greater whole. It tells me, yes, I am the center of the universe. All consciousness begins *here*, all perception comes from *this* source, *this* pocket of warmth, *this* little perfect circle of being, of form and content, matter and metaphysics, skin and spirit—and I no longer feel alone, as if some presence allows this source of safety, this pouch of protection to embrace me in its all-encompassing hand and fend off the icy fingers that seek to rip me out into the frozen cold and toss me before the ice-cube dagger thrusts of brute anonymity and question.

SCENE: *McSween sitting room.*

Stage left, Mr. McSween is sitting at the piano, elbows on the keyboard, head in his hands. Mrs. McSween is stand-

ing behind him, hands on his shoulders. The rest of Tunstall's men (Brewer, Widenmann, Middleton, Waite, McCloskey, and George Washington, the ex-slave, are scattered around the room, sitting in chairs and leaning against the wall.

Stage right, we see Billy the Kid sitting at a table deeply absorbed in cleaning his guns. As the scene progresses he will be seen winnowing his Winchester, inside and out, first oiling it, then polishing the barrel and waxing the wood before switching to his pistol.

MIDDLETON (*leaning against a wall*)
Well, what'll we do now? (*looks towards Brewer and adds accusingly*) You got any ideas, Dick?

BREWER (*sitting*)
You act as though it's my fault!

MIDDLETON
You didn't hesitate giving out orders before we left the ranch. What was that I recall you saying: (*switches to a mocking, high-pitched voice*) "At the first sign of trouble, take to the hills boys." We didn't think that meant leaving Mr. Tunstall behind, did we boys?

BREWER (*standing up*)
Are you calling me yella?

MIDDLETON (*straightening up*)
If the boot fits...

Brewer leaps out of his chair toward Middleton...[63]

But here, safe in my warm darkness, I'm fully condensed into pure being, yet, paradoxically, I feel more a part of the great expanse of existence. It's as if the whole universe had shrunken itself into my inner darkness, been sucked into my being—yet, at the same time, this same darkness, this being swallowed into nothingness, expands back into the universe like a black hole in reverse. Each extreme—the smallest of small, the largest of large—equals the same infinity, each opposite—the ultimate peace, separate, yet so much a part of everything that such words as fear, anger, and pain lose all meaning, as if such trivial concepts are beneath the comprehension of floating souls. Then I feel myself slipping even further away, into a consciousness beyond sleep, beyond weightlessness, beyond . . .

The phone rings, rudely shaking me from my reveries.

Billy, rifle in hand, leaps between the two men.

THE KID
Please! There's a lady in the room.

Mrs. McSween nods back in thanks and then goes back to consoling her husband. Brewer and Middleton regretfully return to their previous positions. The Kid sits, puts his rifle down, and now begins cleaning his revolver with the same methodical care.

WIDENMANN (*with German accent*)
Since eet ees I zat vas herr Tunstall's closess friend, eet ees I zat should take over.

BREWER
I've never taken orders from you, and I'm not about to.

WIDENMANN
Zen maybe eet ees about time zat you *take* orders instead of *give* zem.

BREWER (*rising again, fists clenched*)
Why you dirty little...

THE KID
Watch your mouth, Dick!

WAITE
Brewer, Widenmann, everyone—there is only one here who deserves to be chief.

All eyes turn expectantly to the Indian, except McSween, who has not raised his head from his hands. Waite reaches into his pocket and takes out Tunstall's old pipe. With two hands he carries it over to McSween. All eyes now settle on the Scotchman who hasn't moved. Then, like a daydreaming student who realizes that the teacher has asked him a question, he raises his head and looks around the room until he notices the Indian before him and then the pipe. Recognizing the pipe, he carefully takes it. He looks back around the room and then to his wife. She nods in confirmation. Grasping the pipe, he stands and straightens his jacket.

McSWEEN (*looking around the room*)
When I was asked by Tunstall to become a partner, he said to me, "Alex, if you join my cause I want you to promise me that no matter what outrage Murphy and Dolan commit, you will not be a party to any kind of retribution that goes outside the laws of God and man."

I will tell you now, as God and man is my witness, I intend to keep that promise to the grave. If I take over, each one of you must also make this solemn pledge.

McSween looks around the room imploringly. The men look at each other, all except The Kid who has preened his pistol and now loads it with bullets. McCloskey then steps forward with an exaggerated air.

McCLOSKEY
I pledge myself if it means anything Mr. McSween, sir.

McSWEEN (*grabbing McCloskey's hand*)
Thanks my son. (*McCloskey looks down at his hand, back up at McSween, and smiles awkwardly*)

THE KID
That's easy for you to say McCloskey, you weren't there, were you?

McCLOSKEY
(*gladly pulling his hand away*)
If I had, I wouldn't have just sat and watched.

THE KID (*standing with revolver*)
Why you... (*spins the pistol into his holster*) I do believe it's time to step outside.

McCLOSKEY (*raising his hands in surrender and stepping back*)
Now Billy, I didn't mean anything...

McSWEEN
(*stepping in front of McCloskey*)
That's enough! This is exactly what I mean. If we resort to violence, we descend to the level of our enemies. Fighting amongst ourselves is exactly the kind of behavior Murphy and Dolan figured after Tunstall's death. It's exactly what *their* men would have done. *We* must be different. We must maintain a high moral ground. We must set an example so the people will support us. We need to give them the confidence that when we free them from the yoke of "The House," we won't replace it with yet another unfair monopoly.

THE KID
But Mr. McSween, with all due respect, how can we expect to fight "The House" empty handed. Mr. Tunstall was unarmed and they shot him to pieces. You simply can't fight guns with high sounding words. As for high moral ground, they started it. They have drawn the first blood. The people understand that.

McSWEEN
If we start killing for revenge, where will it stop? The people of Lincoln County want stability and peace, not disorder and violence. The only way to do this is to stay on the right side of the law.

THE KID
But Murphy and Dolan own the law. Sheriff Brady made out a legal warrant and organized the posse to arrest Tunstall. Brady's got another warrant in your name. In other words, Mr. McSween, you're next. We've got to get him before he gets you. It's that simple.

BREWER

As much as I hate to admit it Mr. McSween, The Kid has a point. While we stand around and argue, Dolan and his hired guns are holed up in the Murphy store planning the next move. And Brady's already made his. He's taken over the Tunstall store with a writ of attachment. While we chew the fat, his deputies are feasting on the supplies we ordered all the way from St. Louis so the people wouldn't have to go into debt and lose their homes. While we're sitting on our high horses, Brady's boys are sitting on boxes of brand new bullets. I don't think they plan to leave without a fight. And whether we like it or not, Murphy and Dolan's next step will be to take the fight to us. How can we get the store back from Brady or defend ourselves against Dolan without fighting?

McSWEEN

We must find a legal way.

THE KID

And what about Mr. Tunstall's murderers—is there a legal way to arrest a legal posse?

McSWEEN

Yes, if we can prove that Tunstall was arrested with unnecessary force.

WASHINGTON

`Scuse me Mr. McSween, suh, but they's somethin' I's thinks you should knows.

McSWEEN

If it relates to our discussion, George.

WASHINGTON
(*taking off his blue Civil War cap*)
Yes suh, I believe it do. I's dere tah help lif Mistah Tunstah body on de table fo de doctah tah view. Then I stay tah lif de body in de coffin. I's see dat Sheriff Brady, he pay

de doctah from de fort a hundred dollah, and dat doctah, he din stay long enough but look de body over and say deys two bullet holes. Dat all he see, jess two bullet holes dat kill Mistah Tunstah and no odah damage to de body.

McSWEEN
My good man, do you mean to tell me that you witnessed Sheriff Brady paying the doctor from Fort Stanton to falsify an official report?

WASHINGTON
Da Rev. Ealy dere too. He see de body, but he no see de sheriff pay de man.

McSWEEN
If this be true, the official report will fail to note the full damage to the body. Brady will be able to support his story that Tunstall was shot while resisting arrest. However, we do have the good reverend's testimony. He assisted in the post-mortem. As a doctor, his testimony can counter Dr. Appel's in a court of law.

THE KID
Law, what law? Murphy's got the support of Colonel Dudley's doctor, because Dudley buys his beef from Murphy who steals it from us. Murphy's got everyone in his pocket: the sheriff, the army, the district attorney, Judge Bristol, Governor Axtell, and it's all backed by the *Sante Fe Ring* who lords over the entire territory. That kind of law ain't going to punish the cowards that killed Mr. Tunstall.

The men nod in support. The Kid then reaches over and picks up his Winchester.

THE KID
Mr. Tunstall gave me this gun to hunt with and that's exactly what I'm going to use it for. I'm going to hunt down his murderers, each and every one of them, and I'm not going to rest until I see them in their graves and that includes Brady.

The men voice their support of The Kid, except McCloskey, who has a look of deep concern etched on his face.

McSWEEN
But that's cold blooded murder Billy. If we break the law, we are no better than they. Law and order is what we need now more than ever, or else we will all descend into wild animals.

THE KID
There's no law here, but Murphy's law. Murphy and Dolan aren't going to rest until they see all of us buried next to Mr. Tunstall. It's us against them. I say kill them before they kill us. If anyone has a better plan than that, I'd like to hear it.

THE OTHERS
Hear, hear!
A knock is heard from the front door and all the cowboys draw their guns (except McSween and his wife who are unarmed). There is a heavy pause. A second knock is heard. The men cock their triggers back. The Kid, alone, stands and approaches the door.

THE KID
Who goes there?[64]

Each muffled ring beyond my woolen cocoon, echoes loudly in the cold darkness of my bedroom. The ringing finally stops and the answering machine clicks in.
"Hello . . .?"
O.K. I'm coming, I'm coming . . .

VOICE OFFSTAGE
El Chivato, Is that you?

THE KID
Chávez! Who's with you?

CHAVEZ
Constable Martinez and many other *compadres*

who have come in support of the good padre Tunstall, God bless his soul.

The men lower their guns and the Kid opens the door. Chávez enters and the Kid looks outside.

THE KID
Well stake me to a fill, there must be sixty *compañeros* out there.

The men relax, smile, and murmur with relief. McSween steps forward and addresses Chávez. As everyone's attention turns to Chávez, McClosky edges toward the door.

CHAVEZ
The people have come, *señor*, to take part in the great battle to reclaim our town from the Murphy/Dolan *banditos*. We are well armed and ready to die in the glorious cause for freedom.

Unnoticed, McCloskey slips out the door.

McSWEEN
Chávez, you are a fine and honorable man, but your men have families. Tell them to go home and protect their homes. With the current state of lawlessness, unsupervised women and children are in grave danger. Besides the Jesse Evans gang, Murphy has sent for John Kinney and his Doña Ana bunch. There have been reports that he's turned them loose on the populace. These mercenaries have begun a reign of terror: raping, pillaging, and shooting down all native New Mexicans. Please express my warmest gratitude for their support, but tell your men that I could not bear it if anything should happen to their homes and family in their absence. Afterwards, please show in Constable Martinez.

Chávez leaves

THE KID
Why did you send those men away? With an army

like that we could have fried Murphy and Dolan in Texas butter.

McSWEEN
Mob violence is the first sign of anarchy. A bloodbath will not solve our problems, Billy. Violence only breeds more violence. Be patient, laddy buck, law and order shall prevail.

Chávez enters with Constable Martinez.

CONSTABLE (*graciously*)
Salutaciónes. Señor McSween, *señora* (*bowing to Mrs. McSween*). I have come to see if I can be of service.

McSWEEN
Yes, My good man, you've arrived just in time.[65]

"Hello . . . Hello . . . ?"
Alright, already, I said I was coming.

Another knock on the door.

THE KID
Who goes there?

VOICE OFFSTAGE
It's Frank Coe and my cousin George. We've ridden into town to see justice done. Charles Bowdre, Henry Brown, and Jim French are with us. We've also brought Squire Wilson.

McSWEEN
Excellent, come in. Now we can establish law and order.

The local ranchers enter with the grandfatherly Squire Wilson.

McSWEEN
Squire Wilson, you still have the authority to issue warrants for arrest I presume?

WILSON
Why yes, I believe I do.

McSWEEN
Can you also empanel a coroner's jury?

WILSON
A what?

McSWEEN
A group of able citizens sworn in to take testimony in determining the cause of death.

WILSON
You mean to use as evidence in case of a trial?

McSWEEN
Yes, that is exactly what I mean. We will assemble 12 good men to act as a grand jury and take testimony. They'll determine how Tunstall was killed and who killed him. Then we can legally authorize warrants for their arrest. Constable Martinez will assist in carrying out the orders. You can also swear in deputies, can you not?

WILSON (*smiling*)
I can and will.[66]

Tomorrow, O.K.? Tomorrow, I'll be there.

McSWEEN
Constable Martinez, bring Billy, and Fred Waite along with you to arrest Brady and Dolan at the Murphy Store. Squire Wilson, you bring the rest of the deputies over to serve the other warrants at the Tunstall store. Then scatter the rest of Murphy's men and reclaim the store as our own. Widenmann?

WIDENMANN
Yavolt, herr commandant!

McSWEEN
You are to go to Fort Stanton and appeal to Colonel Dudley. He must be made aware of the situation

here. He must be convinced that troops are needed to prevent an all out war.

THE KID (*aside to Brewer*)
I hope those soldiers don't turn their guns on us.[67]

Tomorrow, I swear.

McSWEEN
I'm going to show my wife to bed. If you need me at any time tonight, I'll be at my desk working on legal papers.

The McSweens exit. Brewer turns to face the newly sworn in deputies.

BREWER
Men, serving these warrants isn't going to be easy. Dolan and Brady aren't going to take kindly to being thrown in their own jail. Any deputy who feels he doesn't have the stomach for the job should leave now or forever hold his peace, because when we start, there's no turning back.

Brewer looks around, but no one moves.

BREWER
Then we're all in. I suggest we get going.

THE KID
Before we go anywhere we gotta have a name.

BREWER
A name?

MIDDLETON
The Kid's right, we need to call ourselves something.

THE KID
Thanks John. Sorry I got all sore at you before. Mr. Tunstall's murder got me ornery. It's not you I'm mad at.

MIDDLETON

That's all right, Kid. Guess we're all techy as a teased snake.

BREWER

Well, now that we've all kissed and made up, let's get down to business.

THE KID

I say we should call ourselves *The Regulators*.

BREWER

Jesus, Billy, this ain't no game we're playing.

MIDDLETON

Billy's right, a name will give us an identity, give others a reason to fear us.

BREWER

What do you think, Frank and George?

FRANK

Billy's got a point. We want people to know who we are and what we stand for. *The Regulators* has a righteous ring to it.

GEORGE

I agree with my cousin.

BREWER

The Regulators... Is that all right by everybody? (*everyone nods*) All right then, Billy, we'll call ourselves The Regulators.

THE KID

Now we gotta take an oath.

BREWER

Billy, we ain't no boys in knickers sneakin' up and down the alleys of Silver City stealin' butter and laundry.

MIDDLETON

Now Richard, The Kid's talkin' sense here. If we don't swear allegiance, what's to stop anyone of us from turning tail and running when we need them most. If we can't trust each other with our lives, what's the point in even bothering to fight? We might as well split up now and cut our losses.

THE KID

That's right, Dick, and the oath's gotta be iron clad. We all gotta be willing to fight to the death for each other.

BREWER

All right, I'll consider the motion seconded. All agreed say aye.

ALL

Aye!

BREWER

Now *I* would like to add something. Does everyone agree that as special constable duly appointed by Squire Wilson, I should be our leader?

ALL

Aye.

BREWER

Then as your leader I want all *Regulators* to raise their right hands (*they do*). As a *Regulator* I swear to uphold the law while serving these warrants.

ALL

I do.

BREWER (*looking towards the Kid*)

That means bringing them back alive.

THE KID

As long as they surrender.

BREWER

I also swear not to chicken out or desert the cause until every warrant is served and all Mr. Tunstall killers are brought to justice.

ALL

I do.

BREWER

And finally, as motioned by William H. Bonney, known to all as The Kid, I furthermore swear that each *Regulator* will fight to the death for each other if need be.

ALL

I do.

BREWER

Now, it's "Iron Clad." Everyone present is officially a *Regulator*.

THE KID

And, remember (*Billy rests his hand on the butt of his holstered revolver*), any traitor will have to answer to me.

BREWER

(*rolling his eyes and shaking his head*)
Did everyone swear? Hey, where's McClosky? That boy is never here when you need him.[68]

Yes, Tomorrow.

Chapter Eleven

"Bilito was one of the kindest and best boys I ever knew. He was not bloodthirsty. He was forced into killing in defense of his own life. In all his career he never killed a native citizen of New Mexico, which was one of the reasons we were so fond of him."[69]

I sit in the living room surrounded by countless years of newspapers. Once organized into chronological towers, they have fallen over like a house of cards in slow motion or time-lapse photography in reverse. I have trouble reading them now. The words grow fuzzy in front of unfocused eyes. The palms slip over pages that fingers barely have the strength to turn. I toss current issues, unfinished, into the fray.

The newspapers have spread across the floor like lost days—the headlines, the top stories, the photos with grinning heads of state—all swim in a darkening pool of faded ink and withered paper. Each day, another house burned; another government toppled; another pocket picked by politicians, preachers, hookers, and other petty thieves. The whole world, captured within these folded pages, delivered daily to my door, picked up by these hands, deposited here in this living room. All these sentences of history, these millions of words, rise like the flood waters of memory before overflowing into consciousness. How long can the leaky dam hold?

I have a chair, a throne of sorts, set up at one end of the room to look out over a raging sea of words. I sit watch, like an old man on the dock by the bay, accompanied by my last box of *Deep Night Double Fudge Sandwich Cookies* and a gallon of powdered milk, freshly mixed. For desert, I have four CO2-powered canisters of *Super Creamy Reddi-Wip Deluxe Sweetened Instant Grade A Real Whipped Heavy Cream, Ultra Pasteurized*. I can suckle them for hours. Four should be enough.

Beyond is a long window, twenty-feet wide, running the full length of the living room. A low window sill—two feet high—serves as a less than reassuring border between myself and the outdoors. If I happened to casually stumble over it, I'd go reeling through the glass, plunge head over heels, and crash through the roof of the garage below into the back seat of some Mercedes or BMW owned by a luckless neighbor. "Hello, Apartment 14D? I believe there's a problem with your car. It may not be ready in time for tomorrow's commute."

> "On his way to *Señor* McSween's house, just a day before the five-day siege, Bilito and his friend, Tom O'Folliard, rode up while I was trying to plow my fields with a riding horse. He asked why I would do this and I had to tell him that all my other horses had been rustled by Jesse Evans and his gang. While they switched all their gear from the pack horse to the ones they were riding, I told them I could not accept such a gift. They rode off and left the horse anyway."
> - Martin Chávez[70]

As the sun recedes behind the building beyond, her red fingernails claw the floor unable to find a handhold on the yellowed pages of time. Each newspaper lies perfectly still, unruffled by her scratchy grip. Darkness settles in over the clumped landscape of folded paper and ink welcoming the cool embrace of night.

So many stories, every day, how can we feel for them beyond the catharsis they minister? How can we experience them with any more *simpático* than a passive audience in the theater? Like the definition of drama that Aristotle outlined in his *Poetics*, drama and comedy purge the self of pent-up emotions. Left to fester inside, such passions would foul the body and spirit to the point of corruption, poisoning the mind and body with bile, or worse, exploding like an appendicitis or a deranged sniper picking off innocents from a tower. Feel for the characters on stage, cry for their pain, help us forget our own.

Bertold Brecht redefined this concept. In experiencing theater, we are merely displacing our emotions onto others, so we don't have to face them ourselves. The anger, frustration, the love needed to inspire us to personal change is magically purged and transferred to distant characters whose lives play out our emotional dilemmas to a conclusion at a safe distance. Rather than transforming ourselves, we feel temporarily relieved until the problems, purged but unsolved, eventually return. Thus, like a narcotic, the audience needs another cathartic fix to hold them until the next crisis. Many who live off such fixes often seek melodrama in their own lives: a silly romance, a one-night stand, a heated debate, hand to hand combat—constant turmoil to mask unresolved issues. High drama keeps things simple.

I notice only two cookies left and save them, a pleasant reminder of the box just finished. I take a last swig of milk, one glassful left, another sweet memory to share with the last pair of *Double Fudges*. Hunger abated, I switch to the first canister of *Reddi-Wip* and refocus on the ocean before me, the air taking on the sound of surf breaking upon the shore at my feet.

But what of those people who live out their dramas in the black and white world of the daily news—are their souls not lost between the lines? What screams are sealed in that silent space between splashes of ink? As I look out over the graveyard of their suffering, the skeletal remains of once teeming lives, I can make out distant whispers rising on the soft magnetic waves of emptiness.

Straining, I detect the ruffles of brushing dust like the sound of blank audio tape hissing through speakers that modulate with anticipation. Slowly, the whispers rise in a strange mumbled harmony, struggling to be heard above the

cacaphonic concent, ascending into the last streams of sunlight as if they could ride light waves to my ears. Like
choppy radio transmissons, broken language and dust particles mingle in a sand storm of reflected light. Voices surge
momentarily above the din as I struggle to pick individual
words out of the light, focusing on swirling dust particles
before losing them in the shadows. What can they be saying
to me: a message, random complaints, instructions?

I suck the last drops of cream from the first canister until
the CO_2 dribbles like the air let out of a balloon. I switch to
the second canister.

Twilight vacuums the dust from sight. Voices abate like
an audience as the curtain rises. An orange dusk frames the
dark blue building beyond. The looming structure spreads
tall and wide obscuring any other view out of the window
spacious as it is. As evening fades to night, it's like an
empty movie screen filled with rows and rows of darkened
windows. As apartment lights pop on, it draws all your
attention. If the curtains are opened, you search for the insti-
gator. Someone undressing? No, it's too early for that,
maybe later. Just people coming home from work: a coat
draped over a chair, a briefcase dropped to the floor—
gnored in the next room by a shadowy figure lit dimly by
the flickering light of a T.V. "What's for dinner, honey?"
"Fix it yourself, I'm pooped—I work too, you know!"

With each light switched on, each apartment reveals a
different life of waking, working, eating, defecating, argu-
ing, demanding, not getting, accusing, sleeping, and waking
once more to start the process of dying all over again—the
only benefit being that, as you get older, the days go quicker
and the sensations of the mind and body mercifully dull.

Third canister.

More doors opening and slamming shut, more lights
snapping on, more tired bodies slumping down in seats,
more beams of infected light streaming into my living room
over the folded pages of this world like stars illuminating
the skyscraper husks tumbled over in the slow earthquake
of time's passing. As I sit in the darkening gloom surveying

my domain, the lights begin to irradiate my skin. Each apartment across the way casts its accusatory beam like search lights locating an escaped criminal and adds its voice to the muffled murmur rising once again from the floor.

I pop the top of the fourth and last can.

Can I pick out words or would the voices find me if I only could relax long enough? Can I will myself into the deep meditative state required to hear the unsaid. Can I calm my nervous heart—give into fear like diving into the wreck? I concentrate on the beating of my heart, absorb its rapid rhythm, each pump, each squirt of blood seeking the farthest reaches of my body—shoulders unhitching, stomach untightening over my belt, head pleasantly dropping forward naturally askew giving in to gravity. I'm finally sinking into weightlessness. I feel myself evaporate into the air like rubbing alcohol.

A voice distinguishes itself from the din.

Do it.

Do what? I gaze out fuzzily over the rumbled swell and beyond into the chasm between this building and the next in whose pit the garage roof beckons. Glaring lights stab my eyes like a prisoner during interrogation. I lose focus as the room turns into a blinding white light. Like a pressure chamber, the air grows heavy, too thick to breathe, compressing me into a tight throb.

Define yourself!

How?

"Yes, the Kid and I did paint the town red a time or two, although I must say that I never did see him imbibe any bug juice. He told me that as a boy it had caused him to insult his mother, so he never had a drop since. Now of the ladies, he did indeed have his fill. It was said of the Kid that he had 'a *querida* in every plaza.' I personally heard tell of Lily Huntress in Roswell, Emily Schulander in Las Vegas, Fredericke Deolavera in Anton Chico, and in Fort Sumner, Abrana Garcia, Nasaria Yerbe, and Celsa Guitierrez, just to name a few. There was a rumor that he was with Celsa's sister Apolinaria, Pat Garrett's wife, just before Garrett shot him. Since the Kid went to Maxwell's bedroom to ask if he could cut a piece of the calf hanging in the courtyard, that would make it Garrett's wife that gave Billy the appetite."[71]

Get a job . . .
What can I do?
a wife . . .
How can I support another when I can't support myself?
a few kids maybe . . .
How can I look into trusting eyes when I can't trust myself?
a house in the country . . .
How can I be a professional, a husband, a father—I can't even be me?
a dog, a cat, a two-car garage . . .

"But many close to the Kid said that he went to Fort Sumner to marry Paulita Maxwell. If that is the truth, I am not surprised that Garrett was talking to her father secretly in the old man's bedroom with the lights out. What father wants his daughter to marry an outlaw?

Pat had two deputies posted outside, but they did not recognize the Kid as he passed by. They figured Billy was Mexicano. By then he looked it. So when the Kid stumbled into the secret meeting, the old man must have been scared half to death. When the Kid asked Pete in Spanish about the strange gringos, the old man knew Garrett did not understand. Instead of answering the Kid, Maxwell said to Garrett, 'That's him!,' so Pat plugged the Kid on Pete's word." - Add Casey[72]

I open my eyes and make out the phantom grey ceiling above. The wooden floor pounds my head. I must have slipped off the chair. How long was I out? The apartment building across the way is completely dark. A purplish glow emanates from the sky above. The newspaper sea squirms ever so slightly. I close my eyes and put my head in my hands. A metallic voice rises over the din as the echo of typewriter keys slap crisp paper.

"Last night's rainstorm claimed at least two lives when a car traveling northbound on the West Side Highway spun out of control and crashed through the guardrail in upper Manhattan shortly before midnight."[73]

Tears warm my palms.

"The car tumbled down a densely wooded embankment into southbound traffic lanes before finally coming to a stop. Fortunately, no other vehicles were involved, but both the driver and passenger, husband and wife, were pronounced dead at the scene. The two victims' names are being withheld until surviving family members can be located."[74]

I wipe them over my face in an ecstasy of righteous remorse.

"They are survived by a five-year-old son."[75]

The phone rings.

Chapter Twelve

The Lincoln County War raged on with a life of its
own. It drained the county's resources, led all the key participants to financial ruin, and left widows and orphans in
its wake.[76]

It was Billy the Kid who first heard the horses, maybe a
mile off. He made out the distant rumbling with his ear
pinned to the floor of the McSween living room. The way
they pounded, Billy calculated, they must be weighed down
with something. In this territory a force of that size only carried one thing: guns and lead. His first instinct was to run, but
they were already surrounded by Jimmy Dolan's collection of
cutthroats. He turned to wake Brewer, then feeling stupid,
slapped his knee. Brewer cashed his chips in last April during
the shootout at Blazer's Mill. Billy still couldn't believe the
shot by Buckshot Roberts when Brewer stuck his head up just
above the logs. Every bounty hunter west of the Pecos had
wanted their hides since Dolan put a two-hundred dollar
price tag on each Regulator. Old Buckshot never collected,
however. Charles Bowdre saw to that.

But who could this mass of riders be? Were they citizens
and local ranchers who supported their struggle to rid the
valley of The House? If not, then who?[77]

Outrages were committed on both sides, yet without exception the five-day siege of the McSween household along the main street of Lincoln in the very center of
town had an especially perverse element.[78]

The phone rings as I stand before the threshold of freedom. I must get out before the answering machine clicks in
or risk ill fortune. I throw caution to the wind, swing open
the door, and leap out. Miraculously, the coast is clear. I
lumber quickly down the empty hall, my rug-padded foot-

steps the only sound. The elevator opens immediately upon my touch. Empty! I take a deep breath before entering to protect myself from foul odors caged within. I descend smoothly holding my breath. Please make it without stopping—10, 9 , 8, 7, 6 (my lungs scream for air), 5, 4, 3 . . . 3! No, it's stopping! Who would get in on the third floor? I can barely contain my agitation. I'm forced to exhale. I hold my nose and breath through the mouth. The car slows and bumps to a halt. The door hesitates, then opens . . .

Billy took his ear from the floor and looked around the McSween living room. He could find few remains of the original Regulators. Middleton was still recovering from the chest wound he received at Blazer's Mill where George Coe had his trigger finger shot off as well. Hiding out while he learned to shoot left handed, George was joined by his cousin Frank after he had escaped jail just before Dolan could hang him. Neither were in the mood for a big fight. Billy's closest compadre, Fred Waite, had gone back to Indian Territory to rejoin his Choctaw brethren and with him went the Kid's dreams of starting a ranch. Bowdre had returned to his wife, Manuela, to protect her from Dolan's raiding parties after his gangs razed San Patricio where her young cousin, Allamanda, had been raped so brutally, she bled to death.

Doc Scurlock was up to his old tricks "recovering" stolen cattle. Chisum's stock detective Frank McNab and poor Ab Sanders ate their last breakfast together, bushwhacked by the Three Rivers Boys who joined forces with Dolan because they hated Chisum for owning the best grazing land. They weren't the only gang to work for Dolan now that Murphy had drunk himself to a slow death, and they weren't the only ones to give up ranching to rustle Chisum cattle, rebrand it, and sell it to Dolan so he could fulfill his bloated U.S. Army contracts. Kinney's Santa Ana bunch, Jesse Evans' gang, Frank Wheeler and his San Nicholas Spring rustlers, Sheriff Peppin and his "deputies," countless bounty hunters and hired guns, it was no wonder that the last of the McSween faction, just a handful of those brave or foolish enough to stick it out to the end, were holed up at the lawyer's house in Lincoln surrounded by hoards of well-armed and ruthless men. Then who could those riders be?[79]

The five-day siege of the McSween household is considered by historians as the climactic end to the Lincoln County War. The war's denouement, however, would last years. With certain participants the war was never over. Many would seek revenge long after the smoke cleared. One in particular, Robert Olinger, vowed to avenge his friend Bob Beckwith killed on the last night of the five-day siege. He placed the blame squarely upon Billy's head, and it was Billy's head he vowed to get.[80]

I'm shocked at her beauty: small, five foot two, maybe ninety pounds, with blue/black hair, ebony eyes, and tanned skin like a palomino pony. An ashen cross on her smooth forehead marks the day. Light wisps of hair float along the curve of her neck as she enters the car without looking up. Turning gracefully, she corners herself. She must be Mexican, possibly of Indian blood. Ah, noble Native American stock blended with the proud blood of *Conquistadores*. The harsh elevator light circles above her like a halo. I try to catch my breath without breathing heavily. As we begin our descent, I melt into the paneling.

The riders were on the outskirts of Lincoln by now and if they weren't friendly, it was only a matter of time before Dolan's men shot them up like snakes in a pit. In spite of the sand bags they had piled up behind the windows and doors, the McSween home was no fortress. Mrs. McSween had gone through great lengths to furnish her home with the style and grace befitting the home of a big city lawyer, as if by example, she could lead Lincoln from being a dusty cowtown into becoming a great metropolis. Now, even the piano that Mrs. McSween had insisted on playing to bolster their spirits, was riddled with bullet holes. It was the first piano in these parts, was it doomed to be the last?

Still, the Kid regretted nothing. In spite of all the setbacks they had suffered, there were also a few great victories. Morton and Baker, members of the "posse" that "attempted to arrest" Tunstall, had got their just desserts and McClosky too, that traitor. Billy knew all along that McClosky wore the Dolan brand and was just waiting for an opportunity to expose him. Expose him he did. He exposed his guts for the vultures to chew on. Of the other posse members, Hill got his while trying to rob an immigrant family with Jesse Evans. They didn't figure on the old German defending himself. Too bad the German aimed his shotgun low on Jesse as he ran off, but with his britches full of lead it must have made the ride home a painful one. Manuel Segovia, that phony Indian, wasn't as lucky. Too bad Billy wasn't there when José Chavez y Chavez turned his toes into daisies.

And old Sheriff Brady was on his way to arrest McSween with another "legal posse" when the Regulators bushwhacked Brady and his deputies right there on main street. All escaped but Brady, which only made sense since he was the only one they were aiming at anyway. Billy even got his Winchester carbine back, the one that Brady confiscated the last time he had arrested him. A bullet dusted Billy's leg on both sides after he jumped the fence to retrieve the rifle, but that was the rifle Tunstall had given him. He'd have taken a bullet through the heart trying to retrieve it. He had to lie in his own blood beneath the floor of the old Tunstall store while the posse tore it apart looking for him, but it was well worth the effort. With the 16 shot repeating rifle, his new revolver (a Double-Action Colt Thunderer!) and his old dependable Peacemaker, he'd either escape or make peace with his Maker trying. He would have liked to finish Murphy off himself if that low-down bone-plumber hadn't drunk himself into a death stupor. Unfortunately, Dolan was still alive and kicking and would stop at nothing until he finished off McSween and every last one of his followers.

But his mind was wandering, what about these riders? He put his ear back to the floor. The horses had entered the town and slowed to a walk.[81]

If Billy had died along with so many others on that fateful night, no one would have ever heard of "the Kid." Yet the desperate boldness that was to characterize his deeds, whether he was portrayed as an outlaw saint or infant rascal, gave ample fodder to the Santa Fe Ring-dominated papers that supported Dolan. Every issue featured tales of the infant rascal's "outrages" against humanity. It wasn't long before the dime novels began to pick up on America's growing interest in "Billy the Kid, the Boy Bandit King."[82]

Carefully, I breathe in through the nose. A light fragrance of spring flowers fill the elevator car. Tightly, she grasps a large basket of laundry in her slim arms. What her foremothers lovingly carried to a river bordered by lush grasses and singing birds, she now hauls to a hot pipe-lined basement in the thundering bowels of the Tower of Babel. Instead of birds whistling in the whispering winds, furnaces and other strange machines rattle and pound. Instead of the sweet sound of rippling water taking her mind away as she hand-washes each shirt with love, washing machines slush soap and spin. Instead of cottonwoods swaying garments tame amid the happy chatter of *señoras* sharing the past as *señoritas* wax upon the future, dryers flop clothes as patrons fight for folding space. I want to reach out and touch her, maybe say something just to let her know I understand, I feel her pain, I . . .

I pull back my latex-gloved hand and hide it behind my back.

Billy looked over to Tom O'Folliard, a recent recruit, just a boy, but at heart a true Regulator. He had drifted west of the Pecos, a small time thief and latched on to Billy with a desperation born of orphan need. It was an act Billy understood well being saved from the Jesse Evans gang by Frank and George Coe when they offered him their cabin for a winter of hunting bear and learning the ways of the West. Tom followed Billy everywhere. No man or beast was more loyal. He even rode with Billy to guard his horse during romantic rendezvous. With a sudden flush of affection, Billy determined that he would get Tom out safely, no matter what the cost.

"Tom," Billy whispered.

O'Folliard awoke instantly at the sound of the Kid's voice.

"Listen carefully, Tom. Tell me what you hear?"

They listened together. Billy wondered with sudden hope if the riders could be his missing pals leading a posse of citizens and native New Mexicans to free them. He listened to the horses hooves for telltale gaits, but didn't like the sound of it. The hooves had a relaxed gait, a lazy lope, like a large mass of riders under control, no rush, no worry, the way men ride when they're sure that the enemy is pinned down, can't escape, and they're just riding in to help finish them off. Only one mass of men rode like that, the cavalry, and if so, they weren't riding in to disperse the Dolan gang which had the McSween house completely surrounded. No, the cavalry wasn't riding in to save the McSween gang from a bloody slaughter, they were riding in to see that the job got done.

"I don't like it, Billy, there must be a hundred riders," Tom said nervously.

"Don't you fret none, Tom. How many traps have we wiggled our way out of? I'm going to get you out if I have to carry you on my back. Do you trust me?"

"You bet I do, Billy!" Tom declared.

"Good," The Kid smiled. "Now wake up McSween, Chavez, and the others. We got some planning to do."

As Tom dutifully crawled off, Billy peered through the window. The soldiers poured down the street. At the end of the long column, he could make out a gatling gun.[83]

Following the fall of the house of McSween and the cause he championed, and in the aftermath of death and anarchy that followed, Billy the Kid made his name. Like a baptism by fire, Billy leaped out of that flaming building an obscure teenager and landed into the history books as the most famous desperado in the annals of the old southwest.[84]

At least Commander Dudley would allow Mrs. McSween safe passage out. Maybe she could even argue our case, show him the papers we got on Dolan, plead for protection instead of attack...

No, Billy knew that was wishful thinking. There was only one law in this territory, and Dolan owned it, and there was also only one way out: guns a-blazin'.[85]

I pull my eyes away and try to focus up at the descending numbers. Nonchalantly, I sneak a peek at the curved mirror in the corner giving me a wide angle view of the car. I see my enormous presence obscuring her slight figure in the background. Although she hasn't looked at me once, I feel she must hate me. I'm everything most base and vile to her: a fat, ugly *gringo* who wants only one thing, and it's not conversation. How can I change her mind? No, it is impossible. I'm not the ideal ambassador to change any Latin American *señorita*'s mind about the *gringo*. I only confirm the worst, regardless of intention, noble or otherwise.

The door opens to the basement. I forgot to press for the lobby and passed it without notice. She sweeps out of the car like a virgin doe. I hear a woman's voice call from the laundry room down the hall.

"¿Quien es, Allamanda?"
"Si, soy yo," she replies.

Allamanda, that must be her name.

"¿Tienes el Fabric Softener con tigo?"
"No, no lo traje."

What a lovely name, Allamanda, a flower no doubt. I must look it up.

"Lo vas a necisitar. ¡Apurate, que la puerta se sierra!"
"¡No!" she shouts. *"¡No, no quiero entrar con este gringo pendejo!"*

Maybe that didn't go so badly. I showed the proper respect by not rudely addressing her without parental supervision. That's important in Hispanic culture, is it not? I suddenly feel so alone in the car, so vulnerable, and I must make a decision. What floor? Any Igbo in his right mind would support my decision to return home immediately. I feel so weak as if my heart pumps air instead of blood. I couldn't bear to be seen right now. It's as if I'd be caught in some foul act. I also have a sudden uncontrollable urge for a cup of hot chocolate with marshmallows and whipped cream, maybe a spoonful of ice cream on the side.

I press my floor. The door closes. The car starts. I stare at the flashing numbers and will them to keep moving. I pray to the Gods as well. My efforts are ignored. The car slows. No, not the lobby! Not now! Bouncing to a halt, my heart freezes. The door opens. The light pours in. Standing before me . . .

It was agreed. They would flee through the back, away from the main military force, away from the gatling gun, away from the fire Dolan had started under the army's protection, away from the town they had fought so hard to save and toward the wooded banks down by the river beneath the cover of darkness.

"I'll go out first in order to draw the fire of the soldiers and Dolan's forces, then you go, Mr. McSween, behind the others."

"If you go out there first, I'm going with you," Tom O'Folliard announced.

"And me," echoed JoséChavez y Chavez.

"The more, the merrier," smiled the Kid. "I just don't want Mr. McSween out there alone."[86]

. . . is no one! I exhale in relief. The Gods obviously support my decision to return. But the Gods only help those who help themselves. I can't risk another close call like that again. I hold the elevator and peer out. I hear the front door open, Tony greeting a dweller. I must make a dash for the stairway. Nobody walks up the stairs in this building, not even to the second floor. I stumble into the hallway sensing critical eyes burrowing into my back. I shiver involuntarily as I grunt open the stairwell door. I squeeze in, the cool air flushing my face, the door echoing shut behind me. Finally, I'm safe.

Now for the difficult climb home.

As they huddled in the back room of the once stately McSween home, the fire strengthened it's grip around them. Flames from the ceiling leapt down upon the floor. As Tom and Chavez waited for Billy to give the signal, the Kid coolly rolled a cigarette. When a flaming board pounced from the ceiling beside him, he looked heavenward, said, "Thanks for the light," and took obvious pleasure in smoking his final shuck.[87]

Staring up the stairs, I hesitate momentarily. It doesn't seem fair that I should be forced to climb such a steep rise. It adds insult to injury now that I can't go outside, that I have to delay nourishment and other simple pleasures. Still, I brace myself for the heavy exertion and begin the difficult ascent home.

When Billy charged out the door and into the back yard, an army of guns opened fire. With both six shooters blazing, he yelled to O'Folliard and Chavez, "Make for the rear gate while I cover you." Clutching Billy's Winchester to his chest, Tom ran for his life into the shadows as José and the Kid lay down a line of fire before following close behind. McSween, instead of using the fusillade aimed at the Kid to cover his escape, waited for the boys to clear the fence before stepping out himself. Armed only with a bible, he declared his surrender.

"As God is my witness, I surrender. Who among you will take charge of this humble prisoner?"

He was answered with another hail of bullets, and this time they did not miss.[88]

Chapter Thirteen

I lie upon a hospital bed in an empty white room. I'm paralyzed. Trying to move, even just a toe or finger, causes me to experience a dizziness that increases the harder I press. Trying to speak fills me with such nausea that I'm racked with the fear of suffocating on my own vomit like a man with his broken jaw wired shut. I try to relax as the violent heartbeats stab my chest with clublike precision.

The manchild enters the hospital room dressed as a Mexican vaquero. I notice a slight wisp of a beard beginning to settle upon his boyish face. He grabs a pillow and lowers it over my head.

The room darkens. I'm unable to breathe. I struggle hopelessly. I begin to spin in a furious whirlpool becoming dizzy beyond tolerance, nausea creeping up the throat. Like a skin diver rushing to the surface for air, my lungs scream to breathe until I give in and they fill with water.

I'm dying. I feel myself rise through the ceiling like passing through a soft cloud. I enter a puffy white tunnel circling skyward. From below a faint voice beckons me, calling me back. I look down and see an old man in a wheelchair. Great-grandfather! His voice gets louder. I make out his plea . . .

"Hello . . . Hello . . . Hello . . . ?"

I reach over, grab the answering machine and pull it out of the wall. I take it by the tail and swing it overhead. It smashes into the wall breaking into shards of plastic that bounce on the floor before settling along the baseboard.

I pause before the sudden silence. Light beams squeezing through black curtains flay the dust swirling in disturbed fury.

AND THE LORD SAID UNTO MOSES, SPEAK UNTO AARON THY BROTHER...THAT HE DIE NOT: FOR I WILL APPEAR IN THE CLOUD UPON THE MERCY SEAT.[89]

Sun streams poke my eyes. Helios is not happy. Neither am I. Fortunately, Helios will soon ride his fiery chariot over the horizon. "The sun is too harsh for men to view directly," the Igbo observed, "so we must interpret the shadows in order to see the light." Man has always attempted to interpret the shadows. Modern man has developed photography in which light is used to burn a shadow on paper in an attempt to freeze reality. This shadow is now trusted more than words. However, according to the Igbo, dreams "are the shadows of reality," and they interpreted dreams to reveal great truths. Spirits, both good and evil, could enter dreams and deliver messages or even possess you.

What would the Igbo have said about photographs? When first confronted with this technology, most ancient peoples believed that photographs robbed you of your soul. Photographs of the dead often do seem to be possessed by some spirit. When I stare at an old picture of a family member or friend, I feel closer to them, sometimes even hearing their voice in the back of my mind—how they might feel about something or someone, or what they would say if asked.

I suddenly remember the two photographs I had just been dreaming about.

Upon his deathbed, L.G. Murphy listened intently to Dolan's rendition of the five-day battle. Against his doctor's orders, the major lit a cigar that Dolan had smuggled in. He washed down the blood he coughed up with his first whiskey in months. Dolan, however, spared his dying benefactor the business books for if he offered him those they'd really kill him.

The protégé had followed his mentor's teachings faithfully and, subsequently, had run the business into the ground. The House was bankrupt. It was a particularly bitter pill for Dolan, still young and vital, to swallow. With both Tunstall and McSween finally dead and no one left to challenge him, Dolan was broke. Without money, Sheriff Peppin resigned and The House was no longer 'The Law.' 'The Bank' closed its shutters to howling depositors.

'The Store' was claimed by the county. Converted into a court house, the old Murphy/Dolan hangout, where many a scheme had been hatched, now became the new symbol of law and order west of the Pecos. This irony was not lost on the local populace who referred to the new county seat sourly as 'The New Law.'

However, Thomas B. Catron and the Sante Fe Ring weren't about to give up influence in the wilderness that they had developed so profitably. They knew that Dolan would be more willing now than ever to compromise himself. Colonel Dudley could still award them cattle contracts for a kickback and also lend a hand with his troops in a pinch. A sympathetic new sheriff was merely a matter of money. District Attorney Rynerson and Judge Bristol still had control over who could be tried, and more importantly, who could not. Chisum, sick with gout and the cancer that would claim his life in a few years, was reeling from the losses incurred while supporting Tunstall and McSween. Suffering even further from the subsequent resumption of rustling, he was scaling back his cattle operations and looking to cut a deal. Maybe he'd even join forces with The Ring to elect a sheriff and rid the county of uncontrollable elements.

There was much opportunity to be found in the rubble of war, and best of all, little opposition. Anyone who dared to cause trouble, however, would have to be silenced and quickly, before they galvanized the war's discontents. Unfortunately, Billy the Kid, was not the kind to forgive and forget. Nor was he one who took lightly to being told what to do. Types like the Kid had to be made an example to others. For Billy, the war wasn't over whether he liked it or not.[90]

AND HE SHALL TAKE OF THE CONGREGATION OF THE CHILDREN OF ISRAEL TWO KINDS OF GOATS FOR A SIN OFFERING.[91]

I have the two photographs before me.

A soft twenty-five watt bulb illuminates the two portraits just dimly enough to make out differences and similarities purely, without harsh light stabbing their features beyond recognition. On the left is a postcard reproduced from an original 3" x 2" glass ferrotype. It's the only verifiable photo of Billy the Kid. From this single reproduction all visions of the Kid have sprung. Writers, historians and film makers have gazed upon it and imagined the man within. Of all the data that has been questioned, debated, revised or rejected, this image alone is irrefutable. Whether we like it or not, all reflections of the Billy the Kid eventually lead us back to this dirty, scratched, reproduction, its features dulled with age.

He wears an inexpensive slouch hat (unsuitable for the trail), a scarf tied in front, a leather vest, a bib shirt upon which, according to experts, is printed a nautical anchor, and a hooded sweater that an old Navajo woman, Deluvina, had sewn especially for him. His dark pants are tucked into a pair of boots with heels adding two inches to his height. Proudly displayed is a watch and chain received from a friend, Dr. Hoyt. In his right hand he holds a Winchester Carbine like a cane, its butt on the floor, and wears a gambler's pinky ring. It was said of Billy that he "could eat pumpkins through a picket fence." The light glancing off his front teeth appears to confirm this.

Behind his left hand is holstered a .45 caliber Army Colt pistol. This led to the myth that he was a left-handed gun, later disproved. First of all, ferrotypes are developed backwards. Furthermore, gambler's pinky rings were worn on the left hand saving the right hand for dealing. No one trusted a left-handed dealer. Finally, none of his contemporaries ever made mention of it. More recent copies have properly reversed the image.

"Billy posed for it standing in the street near old Beaver Smith's saloon on the main street of old Fort Sumner (long abandoned by the army and purchased by Pete Maxwell, Paulita's father).

"I never liked the picture. I don't think it does Billy justice. It makes him look rough and uncouth. The expression on his face was really boyish and very pleasant. He may have worn such clothes as

111

appear in the picture on the range, but in Fort Sumner he was careful of his personal appearance and dressed neatly and in good taste." — Paulita Maxwell[92]

This faded photo is all that is left of Billy the Kid. Not a gun, spur, or saddle survives; not a bone or stitch of clothing can be verified. Billy bequeathed it to Deluvina, the old Navajo woman, shortly before he was to be hung, upon her promise not to show anyone, except Paulita, lest it could be used to hunt him down should he escape. He couldn't have placed it in surer hands. After Pat Garrett shot the Kid in the back and ran out of Pete Maxwell's bedroom with the old man at his heels, Deluvina was the only one brave enough to enter *Señor* Maxwell's room and check on *Bilito*. Although she rushed out sobbing "my little boy is dead!", Garrett and the other two deputies waited until daylight before venturing into the room guns drawn.

Postwar Lincoln County was in a state of anarchy. Practically speaking, both sides lost. Tunstall and McSween were dead. Murphy was dying. Dolan was bankrupt and drinking heavily. In war, there may be no justice, but there is authority. Now, there was neither.[93]

The other photo is of Harry O'Brian, alias Honest Harry, my great-grandfather, who is so old that no one, not even he, knows when he was born. It is said he was already middle aged when he had my grandfather (who died before I was born). The doctors estimate he's well over a hundred years old, but they can't verify his age until after he's dead. Written on the back of this black and white print, yellowed with age, is "1959," a year before he entered the nursing home. He already looks a century old. Still, he stood erect, clean shaven, wearing a Fedora, tie, and grey three-piece suit. In his vest, a watch chain is clipped to his left pocket leading to his right. In his left hand, he grasps a cane with an old ring on his pinky. They say he was a bookie at the track before the state took over horse betting. That's how he got his name Honest Harry. He never wrote a thing down: figuring the odds, taking bets and determining the pay offs all in his head. Never once did he miscalculate or fail to pay on a winner.

> Sheriff Kimball, who replaced an unpaid Peppin, was without a budget for deputies or bullets. Until the Santa Fe Ring or some new benefactor could reassert itself, he wisely kept out of sight.[94]

I look side to side at each reproduction, squint, go in and out of focus, lean forward and pull back. The boy and the old man: how the body sags, the skin wrinkles, the cheeks sink in. The teeth get replaced by dentures. The ears enlarge and drag. The eyes grow sullen and fade. It's as if the whole body just gives up trying to hold itself together allowing the chaos of the world to pull at it until, finally relaxing, it sinks into turmoil and oblivion, never to be heard from again. Unless . . .

The Igbo wore ceremonial masks of their ancestor's portraits so their souls could then possess them. Then, as *egwugwu*, they could make judicious decisions on everything from when to plant yams to matters of criminal law. Would a photograph's graven imagery have reminded the Igbo of their *egwugwu* masks? Could a photograph also impart the wisdom of the dead, or has modern man so closed himself off to such things that he can no longer hear their voices? Does the failure to hear our ancestor's voices lead us to lose all sense of honor and decency; to commit foul and unnatural acts?

> Meanwhile, with no source of income for the hired guns and cutthroats drafted into the war, they turned their attentions to pillaging the land. Jesse Evans re-formed his gang and found easy prey among the tired pioneers straggling in from the east. The Dona Ana bunch (once mercenaries for Dolan and led by ex-deputy John Kinney) went on a rampage throughout the native New Mexican community, shooting both men and children, raping the

women, and stealing anything in the villages of value as they burned churches in their wake. The Three Rivers Boys, who were relatively well behaved, now felt free to rustle as much cattle as they could rebrand without fear of retribution.

Conversely, previously law-abiding citizens now felt free to seek retribution for outrages committed by their former brethren under the guise and protection of war. Local patriarch, Hugh Beckwith, blamed his brother-in-law for dragging one of his sons, Bob (killed in McSween's backyard), into the war. He loaded his shotgun with ten rounds of buckshot and threw down on his sister's husband. He had the common courtesy, however, to tell his sister, as she held his nephew, to step aside, "because I will pull the trigger either way."

Such tales failed to move Colonel Dudley, the only authority left in the territory. His response was to finally enforce Washington's non-intervention directive giving his men strict orders to stay out of civil disputes. He then sank into a drunken stupor, ignored the pleas of the local populace, and patiently awaited an inquiry appointed to investigate his complicity in the death of McSween.

I take out the old watch Great-grandfather gave me as a child. The gold has faded to a dull grey. The hands are broken, the glass cracked. Gone are fob and chain. The lid, which once lifted to mark time over countless days, last opened long ago. If this was the watch in my great-grandfather's photograph, could it also be the watch from an even older epoch of history? If so, how did it get into my great-grandfather's possession?

Today's Igbo save everything. Pieces of broken technology get recycled into all kinds of practical uses. Old clothes are patched into generations of outerwear. Any bottle, can or jar, be it plastic, glass or tin, makes for fine tableware. Old iron is collected by the local "bender" who melts it down into tools. Broken Styrofoam, old light bulbs, torn and mauled linoleum, mangled machine parts, even tangled shreds of hair and nail clippings—they easily find their way to the local *juju* market which straddles a tenuous line between this century and the last. For the Igbo, there isn't an item, no matter how seemingly useless, that doesn't possess some value, or why would it have been produced in the first place? The greater the mystery of its reason for creation—of the space and time it must have traveled with some forgotten purpose—the greater its power for wonder and enchantment and, if nothing else, a fine ornamental curiosity for a knick-knack shelf consisting of alien artifacts from the 20th Century. I pocket the watch as a talisman of good luck. May it guide me to do the right thing.

Recent immigrants, attracted to the West by the government's promise of free land, law, and order, began to flee back to the east complaining bitterly of the outrages and general lawlessness. President Hayes, having won a hotly contested election by one electoral vote (and a minority of voters), decided to replace the corrupt governor, Axtell, with the Bible-thumping, Civil War General, Lew Wallace.

Governor Wallace promptly pardoned everyone and turned his attention to finishing the biblical novel, <u>Ben Hur</u>, his one-way ticket out of such a god-forsaken frontier post.[95]

AND HE SHALL TAKE THE TWO GOATS, AND PRESENT THEM BEFORE THE LORD AT THE DOOR OF THE TABERNACLE OF THE CONGREGATION.[96]

Ironically, the amnesty proclamation seemed to work. With Lincoln County looted out, most of the gangs disbanded its members moving on to fresher pastures. Those with roots stayed, but many took advantage of their clean slates to start over. Most of the Regulators got back to what they were doing before they rose up to challenge The House monopoly. Frank and George Coe went back to ranching on the Ruidoso. Unable to convince his close friend to do the same, Fred Waite left Billy the Kid behind and returned to Indian territory to serve as a tax collector. The mean and menacing Doc Scurlock moved his family to Texas and became a school teacher. On the other side,

Colonel Dudley was exonerated at his trial (which featured a hostile cross-examination of the Kid by the Colonel himself). Even Dolan appeared to embrace a more civilized order when, through intermediaries, he offered the Kid an olive branch.

The peace parley took place on Main Street in Lincoln on February 18, 1879, exactly one year to the day an unarmed Tunstall was shot to death by the posse authorized by Sheriff Peppin but led by Dolan. All participants were loaded for bear. Dolan brought Billy Mathews (who had shot Billy in the thigh at the Brady shootout) and Jesse Evans (who led the sub-posse that arrested Tunstall). Billy came with Tom O'Folliard and Jose Salazar (both had followed Billy out of the burning McSween house). They actually worked out a six-point agreement and celebrated with a few rounds of drink (the Kid abstaining as usual). As they were leaving the bar together in newfound respect and friendship, Dolan got into an argument with Huston I. Chapman in the middle of Main Street. He shot the unarmed, one-armed lawyer for refusing to dance. Chapman had been representing Mrs. McSween against Dolan and Colonel Dudley. His methodology included a healthy mixture of prosecution (for her Husband's murder); civil suits (for property lost); and a letter campaign to the governor, the president, and local newspapers discrediting the Ring. In other words, according to Dolan, he was a man "that needed killing." The Kid, O'Folliard, and Salazar witnessed the murder, but were held at bay by Mathews and Evans who had their guns drawn first.[97]

Chapman's death gave the Ring an opportunity to re-consolidate its power in the region utilizing a spin that modern public relation firms would envy. At first, it looked bad for Dolan. Angered that his amnesty proclamation had been ignored, Wallace issued orders to the military to arrest Dolan for the murder of Chapman with Evans and Mathews as accessories. All three surrendered voluntarily with Dudley providing comfortable quarters at the fort.

Finding witnesses willing to testify wasn't so easy, however. Few were brave enough to risk "protective custody." After meeting with local citizens, Wallace came to the realization that

William H. Bonney, known locally as the Kid, was his man. He was highly praised in the community and afraid of no one. Although Billy desired a clean slate, he feared the local Ring-controlled authorities wouldn't recognize it without a governor's pardon. Wallace issued a 100 dollar reward for Billy Bonney, alias the Kid, delivered alive, although nobody dared attempt to collect it. Through intermediaries, however, a meeting was finally arranged.[98]

AND AARON SHALL CAST LOTS UPON THE TWO GOATS; ONE LOT FOR THE LORD, AND THE OTHER LOT FOR THE SCAPEGOAT.[99]

"At the time designated, I heard a knock at the door, and I called out, 'Come in.' The door opened somewhat slowly and carefully, and there stood the young fellow generally known as the Kid, his Winchester in his right hand, his revolver in his left.

"'I was sent for to meet the governor here at 9 o'clock,' said the Kid. 'Is he here?'

"I rose to my feet, saying, 'I am Governor Wallace,' and held out my hand. When we had shaken hands, I invited the young fellow to be seated.

"'Your note gave promise of absolute protection,' said the young outlaw warily.

"'Yes,' I replied, 'and I have been true to my promise,' and then pointing to Squire Wilson, I added, 'This man, whom of course you know, and I are the only persons in the house.' This seemed to satisfy the Kid for he lowered his rifle and returned his revolver to his holster. When he had taken his seat, I proceeded to unfold the plan I had in mind to enable him to testify to what he knew about the killing of Chapman at the forthcoming session of court two weeks later without endangering his life. I closed with the promise, 'In return for your doing this, I

117

will let you go scot-free with a pardon in your pocket for all your misdeeds.'

"When I finished, the Kid talked over the details of this plan for his fake arrest with a good deal of zest. He even ventured the suggestion that he should be hand-cuffed during his confinement in order to give a bona-fide coloring to the whole proceeding."

           - Governor Lew Wallace[100]

Shortly after the Kid agreed to let himself be "arrested," Dolan et al conveniently escaped from the prison at Colonel Dudley's Fort Stanton. Billy lived up to his side of the bargain with Governor Wallace testifying in the case against Dolan. However, no one ever bothered to re-arrest Dolan, so while Billy was hauled in and out of the court room unshaven, dressed in rags and chains, and guarded by two heavily armed deputies, Dolan walked freely in and out of the courtroom, clean shaven and well dressed. Further compounding the state's case was Judge Bristol who had known ties to The Ring. In fact, The Ring's leader, T.B. Catron himself made a rare trip down from Las Vegas just to defend Dolan. It's no coincidence that Bristol and Catron were both Free Masons, but so was the prosecuting attorney, District Attorney Rynerson, who didn't even bother to interview his star witness, Billy the Kid, before the trial. Surprising no one, all charges were eventually dropped against Dolan as well as Evans and Mathews in absentia.

By this time, most of the smoke had settled and Wallace was already taking credit for bringing peace to Lincoln County in the same vein that he took credit for having saved Washington, D.C. fifteen years earlier during the Civil War. In July of 1864, he had been called upon to defend the nation's capital only to be routed by Jubal Early at Frederick leaving 1,000 men behind in a hasty retreat. Fortunately, the prisoners slowed Early's advance on Washington long enough for Grant's last minute reinforcements to entrench themselves. Now, outmaneuvered by The Ring, Wallace again retreated. This time he left behind his loyal witness to answer for his actions. While Wallace returned all his attentions toward completing his masterpiece, Ben Hur, Billy was still in jail without a pardon. Rynerson was now free to turn all his attentions toward convicting Billy of the war crime of killing Brady, ignoring both the governor's amnesty proclamation and the fact that Billy was but one of a group of Regulators. Billy, seeing the writing on the wall, escaped jail yet again, leaving his own message carved into the stockade.

William Bonney was incarcerated here
first time December 22nd 1878
second time March 21st 1879
and hope I never will be again

Billy, the only Lincoln War veteran charged with a crime, was officially an outlaw on the run, yet again.[101]

To the Santa Fe Ring, trying to regain control, Billy was a thorn that had to be removed. In order to convince the Lincolnites that their man Dolan was back in the saddle again, the Kid had to be made into an example. They had tried peace, intimidation, and the law, but they still had a weapon of which they themselves had yet to realize the full power: propaganda. With a slew of Ring subsidized papers (The Albuquerque Review, Grant County Herald, Las Cruces Semi-Weekly, Las Vegas Gazette, Lincoln County Leader, Roswell Daily Record, and the Sante Fe New Mexican), they could spread the word that there was a new outlaw among us, one unlike any before. Painted as young and ruthless with extraordinary physical gifts, the infant rascal proved an infectious scapegoat. Other papers eagerly followed suit.

Between articles on alleged misdeeds and atrocities committed by the teenage terror, the Las Vegas Gazette presented an ongoing serial entitled "The Forty Thieves," an action-adventure-romance that featured the "boy bandit king." The series proved popular enough to be made into comic books and dime novels back East.

Although the Kid was well respected, even revered in areas immediately surrounding Lincoln and Fort Sumner, outlining towns started forming lynch mobs upon hearing of his arrival.

However, the most damaging article to Billy's hopes of a pardon, was an editorial in the Gazette that was reprinted in other papers and mailed directly to the gover-

nor by an anonymous party. This famous editorial did
more to destroy Billy's reputation than any previous mis-
deed, real or imagined.[102]

AND AARON SHALL BRING THE GOAT UPON WHICH THE LORD'S LOT
FELL, AND OFFER HIM FOR A SIN OFFERING.[103]

EDITORIAL
Governor Wallace Take Note

There is a powerful gang of outlaws harassing the good stockmen of the Pecos and Panhandle country, and terrorizing the people of Fort Sumner and vicinity. This deadly band of outlaws are made up of from forty to fifty men, all hard characters, the off scourings of society, fugitives from justice, and desperadoes by profession. They spend time in enjoying themselves at Portales, keeping guards out and scouting the country for miles around before turning in for the night. Whenever there is good opportunity to make a haul they split up in gangs and scour the county always leaving behind a detachment to guard their roost and whatever plunder they may have stored there. This army of outlaws is under the leadership of one "Billy the Kid," a desperate cuss, who is eligible for the post of captain of any crowd, no matter how mean and lawless. Are the people of San Miguel County to stand this any longer? Should this horde of outcasts and the scum of society be allowed to continue to endanger the good people of this growing territory? It is time for Governor Wallace to act on behalf of his constituency and do away with Billy the Kid and his gang of thieves. He was appointed by President Hayes to bring peace and order to this region. How can there be peace and order when such ruthless men rule the plains?[104]

Gov Lew Wallace

Dear Sir

I noticed in the *Las Vegas Gazette* a piece which stated that Billy the Kid a name given me by certain Papers was the captain of a band of outlaws. There is no such organization in existence. So the gentleman must have drawn heavily upon the imagineation.

My business at the White Oaks at the time I was waylaid and my horse killed was to see Judge Leonard who had my case in hand in order to Defend me. He had written to me to come up as you had allowed him the power to get Everything Straigtind up. I made my escape on foot to a station, forty miles from the Oaks kept by Mr. Greathouse. When I got up the next morning the house was surrounded by an outfit led by one Carlyle. Greathouse went out to speak with them and then Carlyle came into the house and demanded a surrender. I asked for their papers and they had none. So I concluded it amounted to nothing more than a mob and told Carlyle that he would have to stay in the house and lead the way out that night. Soon after a note was brought in stating that if Carlyle did not come out inside of five minutes they would kill the station keeper. in a short time a shot was fired on the outside and Carlyle thinking Greathouse was killed jumped through the window and was killed by his own Party they think it was me trying to make my escape. the Party then withdrew. They returned the next day to burn an old man Spencers house and Greathouses also.

There is no Doubt but what there is a great deal of stealing going on in the Territory and a great deal of property is taken across the Plains as it is a good outlet but so far as my being at the head of a band there is nothing of it. in several instances I have recovered stolen property when there was no chance to get an officer to do it.

One instance for Hugh Zuber post office Puerto de Luna another for Pablo Analla same place if some impartial Party were to investigate this matter they would find it far different from the impression put out by the Papers and others who are out to get me but why I do not know.

Yours Respect.

W. H. Bonney[105]

121

```
┌─────────────────────────────────────────────┐
│              BILLY THE KID                    │
│              $500 REWARD                       │
│        ─────────────────────────              │
│                                                │
│  I will pay $500 reward to any person or persons who
│  will capture William Bonney, alias The Kid,and deliver
│  him to any sheriff of New Mexico.
│  Satisfactory proof of identity will be required.
│                                                │
│              LEW. WALLACE,                     │
│                                                │
│          Governor of New Mexico.               │
│                                                │
└─────────────────────────────────────────────┘
```

106

"Others with prices on their heads
simply moved on to greener pastures, why
didn't Billy?"
- Thomas Milton Seagraves[107]

"I will say that I would not have
hesitated to marry him and follow him
through danger, poverty, or hardship to
the ends of the earth in spite of anything
he had ever done or what the world might
have been pleased to think of me. That is
the way of Spanish girls when they are in
love."
- Paulita Maxwell[108]

THEN SHALL HE KILL THE GOAT OF THE SIN OFFERING.[109]

Chapter Fourteen

"This is the West, sir. When the
legend becomes fact, print the legend."
-*The Man Who Shot Liberty Valance*[110]

I have a new plan for safely making it to the lobby. Why didn't I think of it before? It will be difficult, physically demanding, but I've made a solemn vow and I intend to keep it.

INTERIOR: LABORATORY—EVENING

The *laboratory*, situated in the main tower of an ancient castle, reminds one of a medieval torture chamber. The stone walls are lined with shelves holding large bottles of body parts in formaldehyde. From the ceiling hangs a strange apparatus which seems composed of wires and other conduits leading down to a dome which hovers above an operating table complete with leather straps and metal bars to restrain a patient. Two men stand on either side of the table.

BILLY THE KID
Where is she? Where have you locked up Sallie?

DR. FRANKENSTEIN
So, Mr. Bonney, you fancy my lovely niece do you?

BILLY THE KID
Anything to save her from your evil clutches.

DR. FRANKENSTEIN
Save her? How touching. Do all young Americans have such romantic notions?

Billy pulls out his pistol and cocks back the hammer.

BILLY THE KID
Where is she doc? I'm not going to ask twice.[111]

From within the dark safety of my foyer, I listen for threatening echoes in the hallway. When it sounds clear, I open the apartment door an inch. Upon getting visual confirmation, I rumble to the stairway. The stair door resists being opened. It's vacuumed shut! I pull with all my might, but the portal barely opens an inch before being sucked back. As I tug, I hear shuffling behind the apartment door across from me. It's Mrs. Moss's apartment. I hear the door being unbolted. She's coming out!

DR. FRANKENSTEIN
Ah, you Americans do love your guns, don't you?
But you can't see sweet Sallie at the moment. One
doesn't disturb the bride on her wedding day.

BILLY THE KID
Her what?

DR. FRANKENSTEIN
You mean you didn't get an invitation? Oh well, too
late now. But you can still share our joy. My lovely
niece has found the man of her dreams.

BILLY THE KID
Why you...you dirty old man.

DR. FRANKENSTEIN
Me? Ha, ha! You couldn't be further from the truth,
my boy.

BILLY THE KID
Not you, then who?

DR. FRANKENSTEIN
Who else is there?

BILLY THE KID
No, no, you wouldn't. Not even you could be so
cruel.

DR. FRANKENSTEIN
Cruelty has nothing to with it. My creation needs a
mate.

BILLY THE KID
Never! Over my dead body.

DR. FRANKENSTEIN
That, my dear lad, can be easily arranged.

From behind a heavy wooden door, framed in iron, a deep,
guttural grunt can be heard.

THE MONSTER
Ugh![112]

Mrs. Moss cracks her door open. If I make a dash for my
apartment, she'll see me. If I don't move, the day is ruined
—again! The spokes of her two-wheeled shopping cart peek
out. I must make a decision, yet what decision is there to
make?

Suddenly, I experience a surge of power, an adrenalin
boost not unlike those experienced by panicked mothers
known to lift trucks off babies. I swing the door open and
pour into the stairwell. I shut the door and crouch beneath
the window.

"Is anyone there?" Mrs. Moss's scratchy voice scrapes
through the door and echoes down the stairs.

I hold my breath.

DR. FRANKENSTEIN
Come, come my son. There's a man here who
wants to hurt your father. Come, come to save him.

The door opens. The monster comes out of the dark.
Dr. Frankenstein points to Billy.

DR. FRANKENSTEIN
There, my son, there is the evil man! He wants to
hurt you too. He wants to steal your lovely bride.

THE MONSTER
Uuuuugggggghhhhh!!!!!

DR. FRANKENSTEIN
Get him!

As the monster approaches, Billy shoots it twice, but the
bullets don't seem to affect it. Billy then leaps over the table
and grabs Dr. Frankenstein, putting this pistol to the doctor's head.

BILLY THE KID
Tell him to stop or I'll shoot.

DR. FRANKENSTEIN
Stop, stop, my son. Stop or he'll hurt your father.

THE MONSTER
Ugh?

BILLY THE KID
Now give me the keys, doc, and tell me where you
put Sallie. Hand them over or I'll shoot yer dern
head off.[113]

"Is anyone there?"

My heart beats wildly. My lungs scream for air.

"If you don't answer, I'll have to get the doorman."

The doorman, one of my few sources left for positive
first greetings!

"Meow."

"Sneakers, how did you get out?" I hear Mrs. Moss
walk down the hall after her fugitive kitty. She passes by the
window. I take a deep breath and tip toe down the stairs.

EXTERIOR: GRAVEYARD—SUNSET

> SALLIE CHISUM
>
> Oh Billy, how can I ever thank you for saving me?

> BILLY THE KID
>
> I only did what any man would do.

> SALLIE CHISUM
>
> It's too bad Uncle Frankenstein had to die such a terrible death. Killed by the very creation he gave life.

> BILLY THE KID
>
> Some men need killing.

> SALLIE CHISUM
>
> And everything, burned to the ground. Maybe it's all for the best. And to think that father sent me overseas to learn more of the world before I marry. Maybe there are some things we're better off not knowing.

> BILLY THE KID
>
> Maybe.

> SALLIE CHISUM
>
> Although father sent me here to gain the culture needed to marry into a prominent family, I've learned some thing more important. I've learned that there's more to a man than his title or birth. Billy, you do understand what I'm saying, don't you?

> BILLY THE KID
>
> Yes, I believe I do.

Sallie hugs Billy passionately.

SALLIE CHISUM

Oh Billy, please don't go. I'll die at boarding school separated from you. Let's run away together Billy. You do love me don't you?

BILLY THE KID

There's no one else for me, Sallie, but we can't run out on your father. I've got to go back now, honey. I've got to clear my name. Until I do, Mr. Chisum will never accept me as his son-in-law. When Governor Wallace grants me the pardon he promised, I'll prove to your father that I'm no outlaw. Then together we can return to America, and ask for your father's permission to marry.

SALLIE CHISUM

But Billy, there's a price on your head and what if the governor doesn't grant you that pardon. Why then you'll be hunted down and killed.

BILLY THE KID

Don't you fret now, my wild cactus rose. I can take care of myself and I do believe the governor is an honest man. He believes in the Bible like Tunstall and McSween did and he's writing a book to prove it. He would not cross me.[114]

Breathing heavily, I descend, Virgil by my side guiding me to the chilly bottom. I pry open the final portal, and I'm embraced by the warm light of the lobby. The doorman is preoccupied with a resident complaining about mail service. It's the battered anorexic and her puppy. The little beast nips at my heels as I scurry past. I make it to the street unscathed before being nearly blinded by the first daylight I've seen in ages.

Billy gets on his horse.

                    BILLY THE KID
You do understand, don't you darling?

                    SALLIE CHISUM
Of course I do, my love.

He bends down to kiss her.

                    BILLY THE KID
    I shall return.

                    SALLIE CHISUM
I'll be waiting.

He turns his horse around and rides off into the sunset. At
the top of a nearby hill, he turns and shouts.

                    BILLY THE KID
    Farewell, my love.

Silhouetted by the sun, Billy takes off his hat and rears his
horse. Then he turns and descends out of sight on the
other side of the hill. Sallie, with tears in her eyes, speaks
almost in a whisper.

                    SALLIE CHISUM
    Yes, my love...

A lone tear falls down her cheek as the setting sun darkens
her face.

                    SALLIE CHISUM
    ...farewell.

FADEOUT[115]

    My eyes adjust to the shining world. A car whizzes by,
startling me. Slightly dizzy, I feel the blood rise to my head

and the first pounding of a migraine. Virgil has surely abandoned me, but it will be all right. I'm out and any self-respecting Igbo would exempt me from danger. I must now find a good spirit, maybe a mailman. Until then, keep my head down. Composing myself, I make my way to the store, bravely ready to face whatever dangers befall me.

Chapter Fifteen

The man at the stationery store eyes me suspiciously as I check lottery numbers while eating a king-sized bag of *Twizzler's Cherry-Flavored Licorice*. My card has no hits at all, rare enough, so I save it. Checking older numbers on a hanging chart, I fill a new lottery card. I avoid numbers that hit too much, but find it very difficult to concentrate with that man's eyes peppering me.

> Dear Sirs,
> I admire your publication greatly and would like to add this to the recorded history concerning the southwest's most notorious desperado, Billy the Kid. John Luna, an old family friend who recently passed away, God rest his soul, was a clerk who worked in the old Tunstall store in Lincoln, New Mexico. In the summer of 1935, he made an interesting discovery while cleaning out the basement for his then boss, Mr. Penfield. As he put old books and papers in boxes to throw away, a very old envelope, yellowed and tattered at the edges, fell to the floor. He picked it up, placed it in his pocket, and forgot about it until days later while he was doing laundry. When he opened the letter, it read:
>
> > Dear Mrs. MacSween,
> >   I buried some money in the basement. If I die, there is no one else who deserves it more than you. Dig itup and start over.
> >   Your friend,
> >   Wm H. Bonney[116]

I finish off a "crispety-caramel" *100 Grand Bar* and move on to a "crunchety-peanut" *Butterfinger*. I try to give

the man a foul look, but he continues to eye me unimpressed. I open up a *Dark Chocolate-Coconut Mounds Bar*,
"Indescribably Delicious."

John eventually saved up enough money to purchase
the old store from his boss, but he never found the
buried treasure. He was saving up to purchase the old
MacSween property as well in hopes of finding it
there, but died before so doing. Shortly thereafter,
the Rio Bonito river, flowing past Lincoln, changed its
course and the town had to be abandoned.

Yours Truly,
Patrick Kennedy[117]

I fill in the last number and put the card away. No need
to purchase it. I never buy a lottery ticket. It's a much
greater gamble to take a chance on losing a million dollars
than on losing a mere buck. I've gambled millions of dollars this way and I haven't lost once.

Outside, I'm relieved to be free of the store owner's
gaze. I polish off a *Milky Way* and move on to a *3 Muske-
teers Bar*, "Big on Chocolate, Not on Fat!", but I like it anyway. Relishing the slight nausea from eating too much too
quick, I look forward to the first fresh milk in weeks. I'll
open a quart as soon as I get into the supermarket.

I pause before the entrance. Automatic doors swallow
and spit out drudges laboring with satchels of goods. My
chest tightens.

Chapter Sixteen

"To the frontier, the American
intellect owes its striking characteris-
tics...that practical turn of mind, that
restless nervous energy, that dominant
individualism working for good and evil,
that buoyancy and exuberance which comes
with freedom. These are the traits that
come with the frontier and now the frontier has gone and with its going has
closed the first period of American history."
- Frederick Jackson Turner
1893 World's Columbian Exposition[118]

K-Town is the local supermarket. It's overpriced, but close, though not close enough. Meats, breads, fruits and vegetables—to purchase such items here would be ill-advised. At K-Town nothing is fresh. This doesn't concern me, however. Candy, cookies, cereals and sweets have no expiration date making them ideal foods with which to stock up. You also get far more calories for your dollar. Calories equal energy. Energy equals life.

A gap in traffic allows me to enter. The electronic door opens to a dimly lit chamber of the great unwashed. It's Saturday and the store resembles an ant farm. A large woman, with rusted sweat dripping down her sideburns, shoves me aside to claim a discarded cart and jumps into the huddled mass flowing by like rotted logs in the Big Muddy. Swampish air fills my nostrils like bus exhaust. Filtering in through the greasy fan above the deli counter, the few wisps of oxygen are quickly swallowed up by the rag, tag and bobtail leaving befouled carbon dioxide in their wake. I try to breathe, but can't draw enough air. I breathe deeper, but nausea overtakes me.

As panic rises like flood-water from my gum-stuck feet,

I know only one way to find relief. I brace my arms, hold my breath, and dive in wedging my way to the Baking Section. There, I grab a 2 pound bag of *Hershey's Real Semi-Sweet Chocolate Chips*, rip open the top, and pour in a mouthful. A sweet wave rises to my head. I close my eyes and nod back into its warm embrace. The pulse slows. Muscles relax. A whirlwind of thoughts settle like silt to the soddy bottom of a pond after being churned up by a school of fish. The chocolate melts and I take the first swallow and then reload. Thus empowered, I review my list. Locating a shopping cart, I toss out Pampers and Vaseline. After seizing a quart of milk and downing a few fingers for courage, I head for the most dangerous section of any supermarket, "Cookies, Candies and Cereals," populated by the foulest beasts imaginable—children!

> Veintitres de diciembre, esto fué el dia
> que el alguacil mayor Pat Garrett nos va llegando
> pidiendo a Puerta de Luna su ayuda
> la huella seguiendo de "El Chivato" mentado.
>
> It was on the 23rd of December
> that Señor Pat Garrett rode into town.
> He asked the good people of Puerta de Luna
> to lend a hand tracking "El Chivato" down
>
> Cuando ven Americanos se empiezan a escabullir.
> ¿No darles vergüenza de salir a la partida?
> Solo Juan Roybal salió de esa plaza desgraciada.
> Particulares no nombro porque sería para nada.
>
> Upon seeing so many armed Americanos,
> many young men began to slip away,
> but with gold, the others were persuaded
> to help the gringos hunt and kill their prey.[119]

Children—unwashed and unprincipled, their slimy

hands paw at everything that impulsive desires crave without regard to decency either in manner or hygiene.

> ¿A los mas perjudicados pregunto por que no furon
> a tomar a los malvados que tanto mal les hicieron?
> Llegamos a Fort Sumner cerca de la madrugada;
> para las tres de la tarde nos cubría una nevada.

> The devil he breathed frost into our hearts.
> The moon lit the way with a crooked smile.
> Onward we rode to Fort Sumner in the snow
> as coyotes howled and shadowed us for 30 miles.[120]

A boy of about five with bowl-cut, raven-hued hair is involved in a tug-of-war with his mother. He wears a cowboy costume: black hat, simulated leather-frilled vest, and a holster, hung low, with a cap gun that appears unloaded, praise the Gods. A strain of mucus skids to the right side of his face as if a hasty attempt was made at wiping it aside but quickly thwarted. He struggles to pull his harried mother back into the Cookie, Candy, and Cereal aisle, yet succeeds only in blocking the way for everybody else.

"No!" he argues.

"Young man," I say, "listen to your dear mother. She's only doing this for your own good."

"Oh, are you trying to pass?" she replies sweetly. "I'm so sorry." She smacks the urchin on the back of the head tipping the hat over his eyes. He starts crying as if shot. "Stop that nonsense and let the man pass."

"Thank you so much, good woman," I smile politely.

She pulls the cart from his slimy palms and walks away. With tears clearing a clean path through his sooty cheeks, the little fiend shoots me an accusatory look without skipping a howl. A future hoodlum no doubt.

> Allí nos dieron razón que salieron ya
> para el "Ojo del Taibán" de la manana.
> Con repugnancia a José Gallegos le hizo
> que le escribiera una notita al "Bilito."

In town Pat Garrett arrested Juan Gallegos
a shepherd who knew the "Chivatos" well.
Although it took three hours of rough persuasion,
at Ojo del Taiban they hid, Juan did tell.

La notita dijo que para Lincoln retornamos.
Entonces el viejo hospital para cuartel designamos.
Estábamos descuidados en nuestro cuarto jugando
cuando llegó el centinela y el aviso nos va dando.

Garrett helped Juan write "Bilito" a note
saying to Lincoln we all had returned.
Then we set up camp in the old hospital
playing poker but keeping our guns turned.[121]

There are so many cereals from which to choose, but the choice is clear. At first I have trouble finding it, but finally I spot the familiar orange cuckoo bird smiling down upon me from his perch. The bright yellow beak beckons; the twisted pink-tongued smile excites; the bulging eyes roll as it yells, "GO CUCKOO FOR COCOA PUFFS!"

Only one box left! I reach out to snatch it, but a blood-curdling scream freezes me.

"Noooo!"

I look down to see the costumed simian staring up, it's beady little eyes full of righteous rage.

"That's mine!"

Mrs. Sweaty Sideburns looks me over as she passes by.

"Mine!"

Other patrons raise their heads like cows pausing between mouthfuls of cud.

"Now, now little boy," I reason, "I was here first."

"No! *I* was here first and that's *my* box of Cocoa Puffs. Mine, mine, mine!"

I try a new tack.

"That's a nice outfit, child, as whom are you dressed?"

"Don't you know who I am?"

"The notorious boy bandit king, prince of thieves, marauding manchild, Billy the Kid?"

"No, stupid. I'm Black Bart, can't you tell?" It draws the pistol. "Now gimme my Cocoa Puffs!"

"I was here first. Now run along to mother like a good little boy."

"No!" it screams, the rodent's favorite word. I look up to see an audience gathering.

"Hand it over or I'll shoot."

"That pistol isn't even loaded."

Pouting, he looks down at the empty weapon, back up, and says, "Mommy won't let me have caps."

"As well she shouldn't. You're a bad little boy. Go back to your mother right away and leave me alone."

It starts crying again and yells, "Mommy!"

"Shuss, you little hooligan, shut up!"

It re-doubles the volume, "Mommeee!!"

A couple of stock boys with price guns join in the audience.

"There's your mother." I point.

As it turns around, I grab the box, hide it behind me, and back up. The stunted savage turns back and looks up for the box. Registering my deceit, it lets out another hair raising scream as I toss the box into the cart and make a clean getaway.

Unos salen por corral y otros fuimos adelante.
Cuándo vinieron, Tomás Folliard montaba adelante.
¡Alto! les gritó Pat Garrett el diputado mariscal
cuando llegó Tom Folliard a la orilla del portal.

Come morning the sentinel give us notice.
Garrett sent men across the road behind the shed.
Through the fog came a figure riding point.
We fired upon him as the others screaming fled.

Su cuerpo fué sepultado con no poca ceremonia
y lo acompaña mos pues se nos quito la ironiá.

El tiroteo antedicho a la tropa de malvados
sucedió como a las ocho y salieron derrotados.

It was Tom O'Folliard who felt Garrett's lead.
He fell and was dragged by his horse in pain.
We laid him out with little ceremony
and by the fire resumed our poker game.

Pat Garrett le tiró un tiro y el caballo se espantó.
Supimos que iba herido por el grito que pegó.
Su caballo sacó a una corta distancia
a donde se quejó pues estaba con mucha ansia.

To Pat Garrett, Thomas said,"God damn your eyes.
I look forward to meeting you in hell."
Said Pat Garrett, "I would not talk that way, Tom.
You're to die in a few minutes. Try to die well."[122]

Out of Hershey's chips, I pass by the dairy section and
pick out a log of *Fillsbury Pre-Mixed Fudge Brownie
Dough with Gourmet Chocolate Chunks*. Tearing open the
plastic, I nudge out a thumbfull, which reminds me that I
need powdered sugar. Powdered sugar is one of man's
greatest inventions. It's far superior to regular sugar, dis-
solves quicker—no teeth-jarring crunch on toast or sludge
at the bottom of a glass of milk, and how can one eat fruit
without it? Fruit is always so sour. The only way to get it
down without puckering up is to pulverize it and add liberal
doses of the old powder. Fruits are too heavy to carry anyway. I need supplies to last weeks. I prefer canned pie-fill-
ings. It's sweeter than fruit and lasts forever. Which reminds
me of the other great powders: milk and purple Kool-Aid.

De la casa de Brazil la huella vamos tomando
sale cada uno a su rumbo y a poco se van jutando.
Caminabamos dos millas la huella siguiendo.
Todo el camino del Tul ellos iban siguiendo.

We rested until the morning mist had cleared
to a sparkling landscape of virgin snow,
and as if the Devil himself had assisted,
the tracks of the "Chivatos" were there to show.

Acercámonos a la casita sin tener ningún encuentro.
Al ver las bestias supimos que ellas estaban adentro.
Nos estuvimostres horas en la misma posición
sufriendo un frio terrible y con desesperación.

To old Perea's deserted house the tracks led.
Stinking Springs, by the Gringos, it was called.
Christmas Eve we spent hiding behind boulders,
laying silent and still in the terrible cold.[123]

Oh, yes—*Reddi-Wip*! Only three canisters, I wonder if
they'll sell it by the case?

Cuando ya aclaró todo por voluntad de Dios Padre
siete balazos tiramos al cuerpo de Chas. Bowdre.
Fue el primero que salió cierto sin esperar nada
a darles maiz a la bestias pues su signo lo llamaba.

One "Chivato" did emerge on Christmas morning
and was greeted by a bullet from Garrett's gun.
He fell back into the darkness of the doorway.
All cheered believing that Billy was the one.

A ocho yardas de las casa estabamos agachados
espserando que salieran los "Bilitos" afamados.
Pat Garrett les respondió que salieran todos juntos
con sus manos levantades y si no serían difuntos.

We hushed when from the house "Bilito" yelled,
"You sons of bitches, Charles Bowdre you did kill."
Garrett ordered, "Come out with your hands raised,
or it's lead for breakfast until you've had your fill."

El Charley no más salía pues tenía malas heridas
se dirigió hacia nosotros con sus manos levantadas.
Ya se abrazó de Pat Garrett y el hablarle se esforzó
pero ya no pudo hacerlo porque luego falleció.

"Go out shooting," Billy was heard to tell Bowdre
and into his hands "Bilito" placed a gun.
He stumbled out but could not raise his arms.
He fell at Garrett's feet and said, "I'm done."[124]

As I turn into aisle three, I spy our budding delinquent.
He appears engrossed in trying to tear open a box of *Jell-O
Instant Double Chocolate Pudding Mix* as his mother
regards the nutritional contents of *Aunt Clara's Fat
Free/Low Cholesterol Pound Cake Mix*. I approach coolly,
feigning an interest in canned vegetables. Before entering
his mother's hearing range, I whisper in his ear, "Cuckoo
for Cocoa Puffs, Cuckoo for Cocoa Puffs" and quickly turn
the corner to aisle four. From the other side I hear,
"Mommy, my Cocoa Puffs! The man! I want my Cocoa
Puffs!!"
"What man?"
"My Cocoa Puffs. Mine, Mine, Mine!!!"
"Now I've heard enough. You say one more word about
Cocoa Puffs and it's no more cereal of any kind, ever
again!"
"But, it's my Cocoa . . ."
"O.K. that's it! I'm taking all the cereal back. No more
cereal until you grow up!"
"Noooooooooooo!!!!"

Después de que ya murió tres bestias vimos atadas
y por el silencio se veía que estaban espantadas.
El soltarlas determina Pat Garrett y se sentó
y con dos finos balazos dos cabestros les cortó.

Billy pulled the rope on which his horse was tied,
a mare known for her beauty, bottom and speed.

One shot from Garrett's gun and he felled her,
blocking the door and their chance to be free.

Los "Biles" al oir los tiros empiezan a cabrestrear
al caballo que quedó queriéndolo hacer entrar.
Garrett no permite esto pues toma una mira cierta
le dió atras de la oreja y cayó en mera puerta.

Garrett yelled, "How are you fixed in there, Billy?"
Bilito replied, "Pretty well but we have no wood."
"Come out, Billy, collect some and be sociable."
"Business too confining now; would that I could."

Ya cuando nos levantamos del lugareite frío
pues por poco nos helamos con el estómago vacío.
El compositor se vió en grande tribulación
al ver sus pies chamuscados pero no dejó la acción.

Garrett ordered a large fire built to warm us.
Bacon and coffee were roasted over the flames.
"Are you hungry boys?" he yelled to the "Billies."
"Ate yesterday," Billy said,"thanks just the same."[125]

I find supermarket check-out lines especially confining. It's bad enough being squeezed front and back by rude shoppers, but why don't they make the registers wider apart? Adding insult to injury is the check-out girl with long chipped-red fingernails. Yes, the nails guide her blood-shot eyes while she lip reads prices off the clipboard, but then she has to punch in the numbers using the sides of her fingers in order not to break them. She licks her thumb often through smoke and coffee teeth to count money, separate grocery bags, or to paw food and tumble it aside. She pauses to flick tangled branches of black-rooted blond hair over her shoulder where it lasts a tense moment before snapping back. Youthful, plump and pimply, her body bursts out of a pair of white food-stained sweatpants and a sweatshirt that has been cut at the bottom in order to reveal a bread-dough underbelly housing a deeply sunken belly-button. Although the thought of even touching her revolts me, I am humbled by the realization that even if I made advances toward her, she would shoot me a look between gum pops that would freeze a bear after honey.

As I reach for the last *Creme Filled Drakes Devil Dog*, I feel a rude bump on my posterior. I turn and the devil bites my heart as I stare into the red-veined eyes of . . .

"Walter, you don't mind if a senior citizen squeezes in front of you."

Mrs. Moss wedges her cart in front of me and pulls a fistful of coupons out of her pocket book.

"My, you've enough to feed a small army," she says.

"Just a few minor items. Meats and vegetables are on the bottom."

She lowers her reading glasses to eye my cart. "Who are you throwing a party for, a bunch of five-year olds?"

> Le tocó de centinela en la tarde en un barranco
> de la puerta de la casa vió salir bandera blanca.
> Dio aviso a los compañeros les gritamos que salieran
> toditos nos dividimos mandados por veteranos.
>
> Day turned to night and silent grew the birds.
> The coyotes howled as the moon played dead.
> Orange coyote eyes glowed in the woods,
> but for one pair, the Devil's, which were red.
>
> A dos allí mancornamos a Rudenbaugh y "Bilito"
> con una corta cadena les echamos candadito.
> La tomada de estos hombres muy difícil parecia
> pues vivos no los tomaban era lo que el "Bil" decía.
>
> As the sun rose and the birds returned singing,
> a white flag was seen waving out the door.
> Glad was I for it is a bad business
> to chase men down as if they are dogs.[126]

With Mrs. Moss preoccupied torturing a stockboy about a price, I turn my attentions to the cashier as she laboriously tallies my purchases. Blowing a bubble while reaching over for the next item, she reveals a fleshy cleavage. As a mental exercise, I ponder the weight of each mammilla—no less than two pounds each, I'd estimate.

"You got something on your mind wise guy?"

I look up into the smudged eyes of the cashier.

"Why no, I was checking prices."

"I know what you were doin'. Ain't that called sex harrassm't. Hey Mac!"

A barrel-chested man turns his moustache toward us. "What now?"

She yells out, "This wise guy is sex harassin' me."

From behind, Mrs. Sweaty Sideburns jams her cart into me. "Yeah, he looks like the type."

"This is outrageous, I did no such thing."

"What have you done now, Walter?" Mrs. Moss pipes in.

The mustachioed manager moves in.

"Why Mrs. Moss, you're my next door neighbor, you can vouch for my character."

"I'll do no such thing. As far as I'm concerned you're an amoral slouch and I wouldn't put any outrage past you. If your dear parents were alive to see you now, it would surely kill them. Now apologize to the young woman, so we can all get on with our lives."

"I'm so sorry. No harm was intended. It will never happen again. Please forgive me."

"Listen up, creep," says the manager. "This time we'll forgive you, but I don't ever want to see your fat face in here again. You got that?"

"Yes, sir."

"Now apologize to Mandy."

"Mandy?"

"Yeah, me, you pervert. Say you're sorry."

"Mandy . . . Allamanda?"

"What's this guy talking about? You nuts or something?"

"No, please, please, forgive me. I'm so sorry. I'll never come back. I'll never burden this fine establishment with my foul presence again. Please accept my sincerest apologies. By the way, I need these items delivered."

From behind, I hear the voice of Black Bart, "Mommy, mommy, there's the man who touched me!"

> "We gave our word that we would not fire into them. They came out with their hands up, when Barney Mason, a damned old no-good trouble-maker, said, 'Let's kill the son-of-a-bitch, he is slippery and may get away.' He raised his gun to shoot the Kid, when me and Lee Hall threw our guns down on him and said, 'Just try that you dirty dog and we'll cut you in two.' That clipped his horns."
> — James East[127]

Chapter Seventeen

Safe again. Hot shower clean. Fresh clothes. Noon. Creeping up the side of my building, Dawn fingers her way to my window softly like a swain scratching a lover's back. It's well past my bedtime, yet somehow I'm calmer than I've been in days. An amber glow warms the room as I settle back comfortably into a padded chair and think of my beloved Allamanda.

The eye of the storm no doubt. Four hours before zero hour. Four hours to kill. Yet, strangely, I am not nervous. It all seems so inevitable. Like a death sentence.

Could it be the fresh blood pumping through muscles that had long lay dormant like a recharged battery in an old car after being taken out for a long-awaited spin? Could it be relief after a highly stressful yet successful hunt, the thrill of the kill, the taste of the spoils, the fluffer-honey-nutter-*Hershey* bar sandwich splashed with a liberal dose of raspberry syrup all washed down with a coconut-fudge milkshake? Regardless, I lay a blank page before me, take pen in hand, and imagine my one true passion, the love of my life, the angel sent by the heavens to save my soul: Allamanda.

Closing my eyes tightly, I call upon the muses to deliver a divine vision.

Allamanda,
I have seen your flower
in picture books, but never
have I beheld one more lovely
than the blossom of your eyes,
black as a thousand midnights,
rising to meet mine.

> "The posse drew up to the old hospital when we were set upon by Manuela Bowdre who had already heard of her husband's death. She waxed hysterical upon seeing Pat Garrett and pounced upon him like a panther scratching and kicking and generally misusing his person. She aired her lungs in a local Spanish that I am sure I am grateful not to have understood. She had to be pulled off which was no easy chore considering the care that had to be taken for she was in the family way."[128]

I read my words of love back and feel my heartbeat quicken. Thusly inspired, I get up and rummage around the library for books on flowers. Behind a pile of newspapers, I find them. In the last book, *Plants A-Z: The Complete Handbook of Plants for Home or Garden*, I locate exactly what I need. The flower is more beautiful than I could ever have imagined.

Neither have I smelled
the buttercup-yellow bloom
of the *Allamanda Cathartica*,
but if that scent merely hints
at the sweet fragrance
which whispers your passing,
never could I enter your garden
without swooning in ecstasy.

> "We were having them fitted for irons at the black smith in Fort Sumner when an old Indian woman who called herself Deluvina Maxwell came in. She would only speak to Sheriff Pat Garrett and told him that she had been sent by Maria de la Luz Beaubien Maxwell to ask that he allow the Señora and her daughter to say goodbye to Bilito.
> "Out of respect, Pat did agree, but he took care to have the Kid shackled by the leg to Dave Rudabaugh, another of the

desperados we had captured that day, and me and Lee Hall marched them lockstep to the Maxwell hacienda."[129]

Allamanda,
shall I compare thee
to your flowered namesake?
Your smooth olive skin
is surely softer than any petal.
Your torso curves more supply
than the stem of any climbing vine.
Your raven-silk hair
sways in the breeze lighter
than any leaf, yet your roots
flow deeper into the earth
than the thickest of flushed foliage.

"The old Indian woman left us in the foyer to get Señora Maxwell. She came in dressed formally and took the Kid's hand in greeting. She asked us into the living room. Being full of trail dust, we begged off. Her daughter Paulita came in and hugged the Kid in tears. Señora Maxwell pleaded with me to free Bilito long enough to go into a private room with Paulita so they could talk awhile. I told her how very sorry I was, but this I could not do. Escape may not have been on their minds, but to release the Kid for any reason would not be a wise thing to do at all."[130]

Would that I
could pluck your pedicel
and hold you in my arms for
eternity — yet I dare not,
for I can only gaze
upon your expansive grace
and allow your presence to fill me
with the benign light of silence.

I look over my handiwork and like a silly little child, feel a tear well up my eye. It drops upon the page.

> "The lovers embraced and she gave Billy one of those soul kisses the novelists tell us about. It being time to hit the trail for Vegas, we had to pull them apart much against our wishes for as you know, all the world loves a lover."
> — James East[131]

An overwhelming fatigue overtakes me. I look up at the clock: 2 p.m. If I don't go now, I may never go, and I must go. I'll wait in the park on my favorite bench, the one hidden within a wooden nook, far from prying eyes. It's been too long since I last ventured there. It will strengthen me to my task.

My palms are so sweaty, I have trouble getting on a new set of latex gloves.

Chapter Eighteen

The Manchild and I have set up camp in my great-grandfather's hospital room.

It's well lit, but we go about building a fire anyway. It's my job to collect wood as Billy scouts out the perimeter. I have trouble finding kindling but finally make a pile from old scraps of broken furniture. Billy lights it using a flint and shortly we set down to a dinner of dried beef and beans. I get up to pull great-grandfather's bed closer to the fire. Billy says, "What's the point, he only wants to die anyway?"

"But Billy," I reply, "What if you were an old man, wouldn't you want to be closer to the fire?"

"If I was an old man," he says, "I would want to be dead."

I hear a snap that sounds too far off to be a spark from the fire, but before I can look over, Billy has pulled his six-shooter and is firing into the darkness as he leaps out of our circle of light. Bullets whiz overhead. I rush to my great-grandfather. As I reach his bedside, I feel a sharp pain like a red hot poker twisting into my chest.

"Great-grandfather," I gasp, collapsing on his bed.

"You are a fool trying to save me," he laughs. "I'm already dying and now you can join me."

"B-b-but," I stutter, "but what about Billy?"

"Billy? Ha! Billy's been dying a long time too. We've all been dying, my boy. 'Bout time you got on the train."

"But I can't, being alive is all I've got left."

"Being alive ain't all it is cracked up to be now, is it son?"

Death—blood-choked lungs gasp for air. The head grows light with suffocation. The body stiffens growing numb with cold. The heart painfully measures each beat in time with the slowing of breath until there's no air. Then everything stops, heart, lungs, and I feel myself rising off the ground. My body begins to swirl about the room as if battling death like a fish pulled out of water. This time I refuse to relax. I don't care if I'm just dreaming. Dizzy beyond sense, I flail my limbs against the whirlwind, tumbling over in a seasick spin. The wind howls past my ears, barking like an angry wolf.

"Yelp!"

I'm shaken awake by a high-pitched bark from the ugliest of tiny beasts—the puppy! Attached to its leash, my focusing eyes make out the familiar pair of stiletto heels, spinach-veined ankles, bony black-leotard legs, fluffy shirt, floppy hat—the anorexic!

"Yelp, yelp, yelp!"

From my prone position on the bench, I instinctively sit up at the shock and so scare the puppy that its face changes from snarling confidence to absolute fear. It darts behind the anorexic and circles around her legs, yelping and whining, hopelessly tangling her in the leash. She tries to step out, trips slightly, and her hat topples to the ground. She reaches to snatch it up, stumbles over her heels, and reaches out to regain her balance. As she looks to see what's in front of her, her eyes rise to meet mine. For that moment in time, the kind that lasts an eternity, both of us are aghast at the other —I for what is about to fall into me, she for what she is about to fall into. Both our eyes not only meet, but picture our fate and neither of us are overwhelmed by fear, or any other emotion, save one, and for both of us it's exactly the same—repulsion!

Then the moment is gone. Somehow she regains her balance, straightens up, and puts on her hat. Stepping out of the tangled leash, she walks off dragging the yelping pup.

Repulsion? Yes, I am repulsed by her, but in that moment of absolute truth, it was undeniable—she was repulsed by me! I repulsed *her*! I feel my heart pump and sputter, my temperature heat up, my blood pressure rise to a boil. My clothes stick to my skin as a cold wind sends a chill up my spine and through my pained shoulders. An ugly knot forms in my back and I squirm snapping it out with a painful pop. In spite of my short nap, I feel like melted lead hardening on arctic ice. The wind picks up. Fallen leaves swirl about my ankles. Helios bears his teeth leaving bite marks upon my retinae.

To awake in the middle of the day, how unpleasant.

I realize I'm clutching a heart-shaped box of *Russell Stover Hand Dipped Chocolate Truffles* to my chest. Now I remember. A gift for Great-grandfather (half-priced after Valentine's Day). Great Gods, what time is it? I check my watch, 4 p.m.—zero hour! I must rise and walk, leave the safe refuge of the park, cross the ugly car-exhausted street, and get there before visiting hours are over, but somehow I can't move. I feel, as Alexander the Great must have felt, when, at the very same age as I, he finally halted his undefeated soldiers at the banks of the river Nile, thus ending the undefeated and uninterrupted march of the largest army in the history of mankind to that date. With all of Europe, Persia, and Asia behind and the African continent stretched out before him—the last conquered kingdom at his back and a new unconquered one in front—Alexander did not attack, not because of fear or indecision, not because of poisoning or sickness, but simply due to the sheer weight of his own body. He died shortly thereafter.

With every muscle in my body straining, I finally stand.

Billy 'the Kid' and Billie Wilson, who were shackled together, stood patiently while a blacksmith took off their shackles and bracelets to allow them an opportunity to make a change of clothing. Wilson scarcely raised his eyes and spoke but once or twice to his compadres. He was glum and sober, and not in very good spirits. Bonney, on the other hand, was light and chipper and was very communicative, laughing, joking and chatting with bystanders.

"You appear to take it easy," the reporter said.

"Yes! What's the use of looking on the gloomy

As I enter the lobby of the nursing home, I'm overcome with revulsion and want to back out right away. People walk about absorbed with purpose. I feel as if any one of them could knock me over and then with a complete sense of justification ask me why I got in their way. If they eyed me with suspicion and asked what I was doing there, I'd be unable to answer. But what fills me with the most dread is the old people, some shuffling by, others pushed in wheelchairs by bored nurses, all with faces drawn and sagging, misery etched in the folds of skin, glistening bald patches, liver spots, shaking hands. The citrus smell of ammonia fails to hide the sour, dank smell of rotting flesh and I haven't even entered through the doors into the main ward yet. I instinctively breathe slower as if, by slowing the intake of oxygen, my body can filter out the death and disease, and combat the germs that enter.

"Ha-haaaa!"

It's a laugh that possesses an integrity, a total absorption on the part of its source, that immediately, I both envy and fear the woman from which it springs. Behind the front desk (a raised fortress armed with computer terminals and medical forms) she goes about her business shuffling papers and filling out forms while talking on the phone, to a friend perhaps, apparently unaware of my (or anyone else's) presence. Dressed in one of those generic nurse uniforms (soap opera surplus), her laugh seems in contempt of such trappings. Rather than being defiant, the laugh, spontaneous and without calculation, demonstrates that the role she plays as a health care provider in no way infringes upon her human right to be herself completely. Her job is just a function performed in order to pick up a paycheck and get on with her life. I must keep in mind, however, that just because I can neither laugh so freely nor wear a uniform without having my identity swallowed up by it, it matters not. I too have a job to do.

"Excuse me," I say. She continues her phone conversation. "Excuse me, I would like to visit a Mr. Henry O'Brian."

"Hol' on, Dorothy." She presses the receiver against her fleshy collarbone and acknowledges me with her eyebrows.

"A Mr. Henry O'Brian, I want to visit him."

"Sit down over dere." She points with her head and lifts the receiver back to her ear speaking into the mouthpiece. "So now wha' jah sayin' about Johnny-boy?"

"Aren't visiting hours over by five?" I ask. "I need to visit him now."

"Lawd, can't jah see me busy?" she says glancing at the forms and back up again. "Now sit you down and wait jah turn."

No one else is sitting in the lobby, so I sit in the far corner after bumping my shin on the glass coffee table. Nervously, I fidget through old magazines until one attracts me with the headline "Billy the Kid: Dead or Alive?" Magazine pages are so easy to turn while wearing surgical gloves. Maybe I should wear them around the house as well.

The article concerns a revision of an old theory concerning Billy: that the wrong man was shot by Pat Garrett and that the Kid escaped to live a long, though uneventful, life.

BUT THE GOAT, ON WHICH THE LOT FELL TO BE THE SCAPEGOAT, SHALL BE PRESENTED ALIVE BEFORE THE LORD, TO MAKE AN ATONEMENT WITH HIM, AND TO MAKE HIM GO FOR A SCAPEGOAT INTO THE WILDERNESS.[133]

A cloud came over his face when he made some allusion to his being made the hero of fabulous yarns, and something like indignation was expressed when he said that our paper misrepresented him in saying that he called his comrades cowards. "I never said any such thing," he pouted, "I know they ain't cowards."[134]

Conspiracy/coverup theories concerning legendary figures claiming that they never died are popular in America from Jesse James and Butch Cassidy up through Elvis and JFK. Why can't Billy the Kid, an essential figure in the

American mythology of youthful innocence lost, be raised from the dead as well? It's an old theory and the author debunks much of it. He even points to new evidence discrediting "Brushy" Bill Roberts of Hico, Texas, who had claimed to be Billy the Kid in the 1950s. Roberts convinced many and even earned an audience with the governor of New Mexico who subsequently denounced him in an unruly press conference which included many irate descendents of Pat Garrett. However, the author does concede a ten-point list of inconsistencies with the official story that raises unanswered questions concerning Billy's death. He even goes on to trace possible descendants of the Kid who may not even be aware of their pioneer blood. I clip the article for my files.

I glance at the clock: a quarter to five! I jump up and bang my shin again in the same place.

"Excuse me," I say as she looks up annoyed, "but isn't it almost closing time?"

"We never close," she says.

"I mean . . ."

"Ah know what jah mean, chile." With exaggerated frustration, she takes out a dull green card and fills in the time and date. "Who jah wan' to see?"

"Mr. Henry O'Brian."

She looks up a computer printout and fills out the card again. "Room tree-tirteen." She hands me the card, but pulls it back before I get my hands on it.

"Doncha come dis late again or me sen' jah right back from where ya come. You undastan' dat chile?"

I nod.

"It four forty-five. Ah get-toff at five. You got fifteen minute. Don make me commup and fetcha now!"

> "There was a big crowd gazing at me, wasn't there," Bonney exclaimed, and then smilingly continued, "well, perhaps some of them will think me half a man now; everyone seems to think that I was some kind of animal."
>
> He did look human, indeed, but there was nothing very mannish about his appearance, for he looked and acted

a mere boy. He is about five feet eight or nine inches tall, slightly built and lithe, weighing about 140; a frank and open countenance, looking like a schoolboy, with the traditional silky fuzz on his upper lip; clear blue eyes, with a roguish snap about them; light hair and complexion. He is, in all, quite a handsome looking fellow, the imperfection being two prominent front teeth, slightly protruding like squirrel's teeth, and he has agreeable and winning ways.[135]

I make my way through the doors and into the main hall when a wave of foul humidity washes over me like dirty mop water. The smell of industrial strength cleaner intermingles with the sour smell of death. I paddle down the middle of the hall keeping my hands close to my sides. When I get to the elevator, I wait until someone else comes to push the greasy button. As the doors open, I'm shocked to see a living cadaver in a wheelchair connected to straps and bottles. I can't tell if it's a man or woman. Its head rests sideways on a shoulder with its mouth agape and eyes frozen open, as if paralyzed while staring into the face of death.

"Are you getting in or aren't you," a voice rudely booms behind me.

I take a deep breath. The doors close. We rise slowly. Forced to stand in front of the wheelchair, I feel its eyes fixed upon my back as if it can read my mind, fully aware of my disgust, my fear, and silently laughing at me, as if to say, "You think this is bad, wait until it happens to you!" I turn around to see its eyes staring right up at me. The nurse takes a rough hewn towel and harshly wipes the drool across its chin leaving a red path of irritated skin. Its face appears either clean-shaven or raw as if scrubbed with a wire brush. How the staff must hate their charges. As the elevator stops, the doors take an eternity to open and I stumble out, gasping for air.

The hallway seems more like a hospital than a nursing home. The top floor must be the ward for the oldest of the aged. Although no one ever knew the true age of Great-grandfather (he always claimed ignorance), it was always accepted that he was impossibly old, over a hundred years, even for as long as I could remember, defying even the most skeptical of doctors before they gave him a physical. Without a record of his birth or even his cooperation, no articles could be written on him by story-starved newspapers nor could his novelty-value be exploited. With all other family members dying off and lawyers taking over, he was finally housed here in a warehouse for the living dead, a curio for janitors and nurses, and a thorn for administrators waiting to insert a higher paying customer.

The smell of death is sweeter now, more ripe and sickening. As I walk past the semi-private rooms, a few scattered rolling beds line the walls like cars taxi-ing for parking spaces. Bottles hang with tubes trailing down into the living ghosts patiently waiting for an available space. The doors are left open in anticipation, revealing crowded rooms split into quarters with over-sized shower curtains, closed for what little privacy the patients had left. Behind them I can hear nurses grunting as they shift lifeless bodies around to make a bed or—if the family has any money left to grease palms—administer an alcohol bath. Now and then a patient with some life left in him cries out in pain at a needle or in rebellion at unwanted food, or simply howls into space as if his cries could be registered somewhere, anywhere, if only for the short moment that it echoes down the hall.

Passing limp, chair-ridden bodies, heads tipped back, to the side or forward, drooling through black gaps between brown-stained teeth, arms fallen over wheels, lifeless fingers resting precariously between spokes, the only movements are from countless pairs of yellow eyes transfixed upon the stranger in their mist. As I shudder past each, I feel as if, with the last of its strength, a hand will latch on to the scruff on my neck and shout, "O.K., that's far enough, you fake, you phony, you false pretender. We know why you're really here!"

Then, looking around the placita, Bonney asked "Is the jail in Sante Fe any better than this?"
This seemed to bother him considerably, for, as he

explained, "this is a terrible place to put a fellow in." He put the same question to everyone who came near him and when he learned that there was nothing better in store for him, he shrugged his shoulders and said something about putting up with what he had to.[136]

His door, like all the others, is propped open. I pause and take a deep breath, regretting it immediately as I fight back a dry heave. I take one latex glove off, reach into my pocket and clasp the battered old watch he gave me. Dear Gods, give me strength. Quickly, I squeeze back into the glove.

I peer into his room: white curtains, closed, let in a diffused pale light. A soiled disposable diaper, apparently rinsed out, dries on the heater. Peeking around the corner, I tip-toe in, hands holding my stomach, and see his feet first, knobby knees, sunken stomach, T-bone chest, blotchy beard, skeletal face, eyes half closed—and experience the shudder of recognition. This wrinkled mummy, could this really be Great-grandfather?

I'm suddenly overcome with the same dread as one, who upon seeing a dead body, is afraid to get too close for fear it could still reach out and grab him. Then I notice his left wrist. It's strapped to the roll guard on the left side of his bed. The leather restraint has a lock. Half aghast at the human rights violation and half reassured for my safety, I walk around his bed. The aged oak dresser along the opposite wall is the only piece of real furniture, likely the last of its type in the building. It's far too heavy to move until absolutely necessary and fully appropriate for the floor's last private room, a testament for this final survivor from an age when the dying were still allowed a few tokens of humanity. A large white notecard is taped to the middle of the mirror, upon which is written in big neat block letters, my telephone number. Beneath the number in smaller letters is my name. However, my name is written clumsily in a different pen as if added hastily at a later date with a mixture of frustration and angry surrender to forgetfulness: evidence of a time when attempts were still being made to speak to the future, to the self soon to be a total stranger.

Photographic portraits, wedged tightly between the mirror and frame, surround my phone number. These ancestral faces must have watched him countless years as he shuffled within the small confines of his cell until finally one day he could no longer rise to meet them. Yellowed and curling, I can make out faded blue pen marks designating their identities, names I've either forgotten or refuse to remember, until I come to my father and mother staring at me accusingly. Even in their wedding clothes, they stare into the camera somberly. It's as if they're looking straight ahead into the future at me (the last active survivor of a broken family wheel) with utter disappointment.

"Ugh!"

The noise sends an electric shock through my back, heart and stomach. I weave around and see my great-grandfather in the same position. Shaken, yet strangely relieved to have the stillness broken, I pass over to a chair by his bedside. Above the phone, my home number is pasted again, this time nameless. The final link to his past left unmarked and forgotten, but not ignored. Tempted to rip it down, I resist, swallowing my shame.

I lean over and whisper, "Great-grandfather?"

> A final stroke of the hammer cut the last rivet in the bracelets, and they clanked on the pavement as they fell.
> Bonney straightened up and then rubbing his wrists where the sharp edged irons chaffed him, said: "I don't suppose you fellows would believe it, but this is the first time I ever had bracelets on. But many another fellow had them on, too." As they led Bonney back down into the cold darkness of his basement cell, he turned and looked back and explained: "They say a fool for luck and a poor man for children. Garrett takes them all in."[137]

"Great-grandfather . . . hello . . . can you hear me?"

His head turns slightly, eyes half open. "*¿Chávez?*"

"I'm not the attendant. It's me, Walter, your great-grandson."

"Great-grandson? Nah, not a chance. I'm only sixty-seven."

"No Great-grandfather, you're over a hundred."

"A hundred? Son, don't stretch an old man's blanket. Nobody lives that long, not even Mexicans and Indians. What did you say your name was?"

"Walter, the son of the son of . . ."

"Well, grandson, whoever you are, corral that talking wire." He shakes a bony finger at the phone, then points to my number pinned above. "Dial that number." I hesitate. "You hog-tied? Go on, dial it."

"But Great-grandfather, why?"

"Because . . . because, I say so."

I dial. My answering machine kicks in. "Nobody's home, Great-grandfather."

"Oh yes they are. Was it picked up?"

"Well, yeah, sort of, but . . ."

"Good lord, son, then say hello!"

"Hello? Nobody answers."

"Maybe they have sand in their ears. Say it again."

"Hello . . . ?"

"Keep saying it until they hear you."

I obey.

"Hello . . . Hello . . . Hello . . . ?"

We saw them again at the depot when the crowd presented a really war-like appearance. Leaning out of one of the windows of the train car, he talked casually with us as the rumblings of the crowd grew spirited.

"I don't blame you for writing of me as you have. You had to believe others' stories, but I don't know as anyone would believe anything good of me, anyway," he said. "I wasn't the leader of any gang. I was for Billy all the time. I made my living gambling but that was the only way I could live. They wouldn't let me settle down; if they had I wouldn't be here today," he held up his right arm on which was the bracelet. "Chisum got me into all this trouble and wouldn't help me out. We used to do business together, but I guess I remind him of a time he'd rather forget."[138]

I look over. He's fallen back asleep. Eyes sunken in,

hollow cheeks, skin wrinkled like a closed accordion, he could die before me and I couldn't tell the difference.

"Great-grandfather?"

"Huh . . ."

"There's still no answer, Great-grandfather."

"*¿Quien es?*"

"What?"

"*¿Quien es, Chávez? ¿Has venido a liberar tu amigo?*"

"I'm not Chávez, Great-grandfather. I'm . . ."

"What did you call me? Are you family?"

"Yes."

"Then please, I appeal for succor."

"Anything, Great-grandfather."

"Is my dresser still there?"

"Yes."

"Go over there. Open the bottom drawer."

I open a drawer full of yellowed boxer shorts.

"Do you not see it?"

"See what?"

"What's hidden there?"

"But Great-grandfather, there's nothing here but dirty old underwear."

"That's it!"

"That's what?"

"*That* is the hidden treasure."

"What treasure?"

"See, I fooled you too. I fooled them all!" he exclaims with a toothless smile. "That's not just underwear, son," he winks. "That's $100,000 underwear—worth its weight in gold!"

The prospects of a fight at the train station exhilarated him, and he bitterly bemoaned being chained. "If I only had my Winchester, I'd lick the whole crowd," was his confident comment on the strength of the attack party. He sighed and sighed again for a chance to take a hand in the fight, and the burden of his desire was to be set free to fight on the side of his captors as soon as he should smell powder.

As the authorities calmed the anxious crowd, the

Kid fashioned his fingers into a make-believe pistol and peppered away at a group of small boys hiding behind the legs of their elders. The young innocents returned fire, one scoring a hit on the Kid's shoulder. As the train rolled out, he lifted his hat and invited us to call and see him in Sante Fe, calling out "Adios!"[139]

Grasping to my breast the heart-shaped box of chocolate truffles I intended to give Great-grandfather, I step out of the entrance of the nursing home, shocked at the deepening gloom of evening. The sun has set and instead of being warmly wrapped beneath my bed covers, pleasantly diving in and out of the last sleep, I'm hurling into the second day without proper rest, hopelessly vulnerable to all kinds of foulness in the night air. Still, I take a deep breath of the cold, the first full swallow I've taken in an hour. A hint of foulness from the nursing home kitchen gives me a slight shiver, yet the outside air, after being in the depths of Hades for so long, has a dizzying, yet euphoric effect on me. In a moment of absolute clarity, I make the most important decision of my life. There is no alternative and the time to act is now. I know I must put Great-grandfather out of his misery.

AND AARON SHALL BRING THE BULLOCK OF THE SIN OFFERING, WHICH IS FOR HIMSELF, AND SHALL MAKE AN ATONEMENT FOR HIMSELF, AND FOR HIS HOUSE, AND SHALL KILL THE BULLOCK OF THE SIN OFFERING WHICH IS FOR HIMSELF.[140]

"While waiting for a train south to Albuquerque at the Bernalillo station, I watched the northbound Santa Fe train pull into the station. To my surprise, I spied William H. Bonney in irons through the Pullman window surrounded by an armed guard. I had first met the noted outlaw in Tascosa a couple of years back where I had lost a bet with the Kid and almost lost my life.

"It was at a dance that the native New Mexicans called *bailes*. This one was sponsored by the Romero family, who could

161

trace their blood back to the *Conquistadores*. Billy and I got on immediately having had mutual acquaintances in Texas. Overheated from dancing, the friendly youth invited me outside to take in the cool night air. We walked across the plaza so he could check on his *compadres'* horses. I told him that I admired his animal, an Arabian of fine stock. The Kid said that he admired my watch attached to a fob and chain. 'Well, I cannot lie Billy,' I replied. 'when I bought it I paid double, believing it was gold, but it does tell time real well. How about a trade?'

"'My horse is worth twice as much as that old watch,' replied the Kid, 'but if you would like, we could wager on a little foot race back to the ballroom. Can a straight-legged city doctor beat a bowl-legged cowboy?'

"Normally, I am not a gambling man, but feeling my blood warmed from the tequila, which the locals call tarantula juice, and noting that Billy wore large boots while I wore shoes, I accepted the challenge. The Kid passed me near the end, but in so doing, tripped over the doorway and fell into the ballroom. Alarmed and fearing for the Kid's safety, his four *compadres*, John Middleton, Tom O'Folliard, Fred Waite, and José Chávez y Chávez, formed a protective wall around him and drew their pistols on me. Billy laughed heartily and said it was all right. Happily, I gave Billy my watch and chain, but Señor Romero, not amused in the least, forbade the *Bilitos,* as he called them, from ever attending one of his *bailes* again for they had carried firearms in violation of the accepted practice at all such dances. In spite of it being worth double the watch, Billy ended up giving me the horse anyway even filling out a bill of sale so I could not be arrested for horse theft. In return, I promised him free medical advice although I do not recall him ever asking. I had never seen, nor seen since, a more fit young man.

"Upon seeing the Kid again, I had mixed feelings for I had not heard of his arrest. Still, I did not hesitate climbing aboard the train. The guards let me see Billy, but only for a minute. A Deputy, Bob Olinger, said, 'I'm timing you doctor,' and pulled out his watch. I recognized my old watch immediately."[141]

When the stern men hired to guard the outlaw lad posed for a portrait, Bob Olinger was so large and muscular, that he had to sit upon a stool in the middle of the other deputies in order to keep his head in range of the camera.[142]

"'Is there anything I can do to make you more comfortable, Billy?' I asked.

"'Sure, Doc,' the Kid replied with a smile. 'Just grab Bob's gun and hand it over for a moment.'

"'My boy,' Deputy Olinger spat back lowering his double-barreled shotgun to the Kid's chest, 'you had better tell your friend goodbye. Your days are short.'

"'Oh I don't know,' the Kid winked at me. 'There's many a slip 'twixt the cup and lip.'

"I never did see my good friend again, nor my old watch, but I read the newspaper account detailing the Kid's escape from the Lincoln County Jail. When I got to the part about how Billy had paid Olinger back with two barrels of buckshot from the deputy's own gun, I laughed aloud and said to those within earshot 'There's a cursed watch if I ever saw one: whoever acquires it, pays double.'"

- Dr. Henry Hoyt[143]

AND HE THAT LET GO THE GOAT FOR THE SCAPEGOAT SHALL WASH HIS

CLOTHES, AND BATHE HIS FLESH IN WATER AND AFTERWARD COME INTO THE CAMP.[144]

Evening turns to darkness. My ankles feel as if they might crumble at any second. Searing shocks of pain accompany each step. My knees buckle with every bump and curb, my back ready to snap in half at the slightest brushback by a passing pedestrian. Distrustful eyes glare at me as I clutch my box of truffles in pain. Cars aim for me as I cross the street. The doorman is mercifully distracted as I walk through an empty lobby. In the elevator, however, Allamanda is there, laundry in one arm, her employer's baby in the other. She ignores me, but the baby stares at me as if I'm Big Bird's evil twin. As Allamanda leaves, my heart shudders with longing. Why did I not offer her the box of Valentine candies?

> "Two candi hearts given me by Willie Bonney on the22nd of August."
> - Sallie Chisum[145]

No, the time is not right—not yet. She hasn't even seen the poem that has immortalized her beauty. However, I am emboldened with my fearless new decision. It's the type of resolution made by those who win the hands of women like Allamanda—the brave lions who sleep with gentle lambs.

AND THE BULLOCK FOR THE SIN OFFERING, AND THE GOAT FOR THE SIN OFFERING, WHOSE BLOOD WAS BROUGHT IN TO MAKE ATONEMENT IN THE HOLY PLACE, SHALL ONE CARRY FORTH WITHOUT THE CAMP; AND THEY SHALL BURN IN THE FIRE THEIR SKINS, AND THEIR FLESH, AND THEIR DUNG.[146]

Germs crawl beneath my clothes. I barely make it out of the elevator before the doors close. The hallway seems a mile long, but a bath and redemption await me.

AND HE THAT BURNETH THEM SHALL WASH HIS CLOTHES, AND BATHE HIS FLESH IN WATER AND AFTERWARD HE SHALL COME INTO THE CAMP.[147]

Chapter Nineteen

"What was it about this killer of men, this pariah of society, this product of Bowery slum and Western lawlessness that has made him the object of such wide and undimming interest?"[148]

Shedding clothes in disgust, I draw a hot bath and scrub disease and infestation from my skin. I draw a second bath to fully rinse myself. With a fresh pair of surgical gloves, I lift the infected clothes into the tub and add bubble bath and a dash of bleach.

Beely thee Keed, está muy hombre. All Mexican peepul heez amigos. He steal from el rico an' give to el pobre. That Beely, hee small like muchacho, but cajónes, I yi yi! El Keed cajónes beeg as el toro bravo, thee fighting bull. An' thee señoritas — ieee! They love thee Keed mucho grande. Thee Keed bee tough with thee muchachos, but tender with thee muchachas. There bee many a maiden with heart saved for heem.

El Chivato heez called, an' like thee beely goat, hee gentle, but no get heem irritado. Then hee butt heads with any man, sin temor, without fear. ¡An' loyal! Hee always help thee amigo in need. Just ask José Chávez y Chávez. Hee bee muerto, dead, had Beely not help heem. ¿Have you heard thee story of how El Chivato save heem?[149]

As I walk into the kitchen to indulge in the supplies I had sacrificed so much to acquire, I'm taken by the light. The midday sun floods the apartment overwhelming my senses. I've had enough light for the day. I should be in bed asleep, but find myself oddly energetic in spite of my exhaustion—wired-tired, you might say. After fixing myself a *Hershey Bar* fluffer-honey-nutter sandwich and a large glass of milk with vanilla ice cream, I settle down in my throne overlooking my newspaper domain. I have so much time to kill before tomorrow, yet I dare not sleep.

El Chivato, San Bilito Bandito, hee thee best three-card monte dealer, west of thee Pecos, south of thee Rio Grande. When El Keed shuffle thee cards, no one ever fine thee queen. Hee an' Chavez, they partner, el compañeros jugador. When El Keed deal three-card monte, Chávez play heez geetar an' sing. Chávez gather thee crowd an' beezy thee players while Beely, hee move thee cards. If there bee trouble, Chávez six-shooter, hee pull an' cock.

One day, they work on Tunstall ranch, el norte in Nuevo Mexico, an' El Chivato, hee hear of thee Chávez arrest for dueling south of thee border in Zaragoza. Eet was there Chávez gamble away mucho dinero from thee hombres, so they gather in thee town plaza with mucho rope. Beely ride heez coballo blanco 130 mile of rough terrain. Hee cross thee muddy Rio Grande, an' arrive by meednight.

Beely, hee not know well thee town Zaragoza, an thee night, eet bee negro mucho, so hee listen for thee playing of geetar by Chávez. That bee how El Keed, hee fine heez compadre. Hee wake thee jailer and say in thee tongue of Espana fluente, "I bee el policía federales with dos gringos prisioneros." When thee guard unlock thee jail, hee get thee six-shooter shove in thee stomach. That night they cross thee Rio Grande on Beely's caballo blanco. Next day they play three-card monte in El Paso until they earn enough dinero to buy Chávez his own caballo an' ride back to Fort Sumner in time to take thee hot bath and dress for Señor Pete Maxwell an' heez Saturday night baile. Beely, hee dance weeth all thee señoritas an' Chávez, hee play geetar an' sing. All thee peepul happy to see El Chivato, San Bilito Bandito, back again.[150]

As soon as I finish eating, I'm overcome with fatigue. The sun reflects off the building beyond, each flash of light a dagger in my tired eyes. Each apartment (quietly critical by the light of the moon) objects loudly to my existence in the harsh definition of high noon. I've had enough of these people telling me what to do, frowning upon my actions, who are they to judge me, me, a soul who bothers no one, one who only seeks to exist at the most modest of levels, who only wishes to be left alone, but isn't even allowed to leave his home in peace long enough to gather the simplest of sustenance with which to sustain this meager life? How can I be more humble before the Gods than I have become, yet they award me with countless prying eyes.

Searchlights constantly seek me out during the night and spy on me all day, continually criticizing, condemning, doubting my very worth. But I can fight back. I can use their words, their pitiful lives, their own stories of madness and murder to quiet them. I can get the final revenge, snuff them out, silence them for all time. I feel my mind racing now. Eye-prying sun-streaks knife through slices of shade. Devil's snowflakes dance in the flames. I know exactly what to do and I'm going to do it right now. I stand up.

> Everybody like Beely the Keed. Su vista penetrava al corazón de toda la gente. His face went to everybody's heart.[151]

Newspapers rise again in triumph, each fitting neatly atop the other. Like an expert brick mason, I rebuild the walls of Troy. Each section of paper rises to block another slice of sinister light. It takes hours, but as the last sliver of sun sets behind the evil building facing me, the last newspaper fits neatly into place blocking out all the apartments completely.

Now, no one can see me. All the leaks are plugged. I can think clearly again. I haven't slept since the park bench, but I'm too tired to give in. If sleep drags me under again, I'll only wake gasping for air, if I wake at all, and I can't afford that, not now, now that I have something to do, something that must be done, a mission, a purpose.

Mr. Smith, My Dear Sir:

I was surprised to hear from you, but am always glad to hear from those who had a good feeling for the Kid.

I can tell you this about him, that he killed several of the most noted outlaws that ran in this part of New Mexico. All of the men he killed got just what was coming to them. I never knew him to shoot a man in the back.

That he ever killed as many men as he is blamed for, or ever killed for money is absurd. He never seemed to care for money, except to buy cartridges with; then he would much prefer to gamble for them straight. Cartridges were scarce, and he always used about ten times as anyone else . Billy was the best shot with a six-shooter I ever saw.

He would go to the bar with anyone, but I never saw him drink a drop. Always in a good humor and ready to do a kind act to some one. Billy never talked much of the past; he was always looking into the future, although he often talked of his mother.

He was a wonder and you would have been proud to know him better.

As Ever,
Frank B. Coe[152]

A reason to live or die—kill or be killed.

Chapter Twenty

"There were no bounds to his gen-
erosity. Friends, strangers, and even his
enemies, were welcome to his money, his
horse, his clothes, or anything else of
which he happened at the time to be possessed. The aged, the poor, the sick, the
unfortunate and helpless never appealed to
Billy in vain for succor."
- Sheriff Patrick F. Garrett
the man who shot him in the back[153]

Armed with my list, I'm outside again. I was up all
night going over the plan. I had one close call, passing out
for a minute and waking up gasping for air, but I have no
need for sleep. I'm buzzing. On the outside, the dawn is so
strange. It lifts the eyelids just as the dusk lowers them.
How long has it been, since the sun's morning kiss graced
my cheek? The solstice sun shines with shocking brightness
whispering the false promise of an early spring as if the
Gods themselves smile down upon my noble quest. Zephyr
blesses me, blowing clean my matted hair. Although the
Igbo may not agree, if you don't sleep, strangers can't sub-
vert you, because your luck is leftover from the previous
day. An aura of good fortune, like a force field, surrounds
me. I feel it vibrating.

I check the list.

A man on foot is no man at all.[154]

I enter the lot. A sea of used cars flashes diamonds in
the bright sun. I'm a little woozy from lack of sleep, yet
paradoxically, I feel extra sharp, as if in tune with both the
metaphysical and natural world simultaneously. My senses
reach beyond normal parameters of perception. The musty
smell of leaked oil and radiator fluid is sucked up by trees

straining to purify the exhaust-saturated air. I can hear the hum of their little systems working overtime. The sound from the highway thrush of speeding cars is filtered through their rotting leaves as my soles crackle loose pebbles freeing themselves from the chipped asphalt tarmac upon which hundreds of cars float uneasily flayed by the wind. Each car grabs my attention as I walk past. They reach out and speak to me. An aged Impala, "Buy me!" A rusted Subaru with four-wheel drive, "No, me!" A late model Toyota Celica Hatchback, "Not that pile of junk, his former owner was a lush and cracked him up. Just look under the hood. Look at the paint smudges on the engine. It's a chronicle of the countless paint jobs it took to hide each accident. Now if you look under my hood . . ."

I commune with the cars. I must know them *before* the salesman spins his web upon me and I'm no longer unable to tell Adam from Eve.

Then I see her.

She's a redhead. Blood red. A convertible, with the top down to greet the rising sun. An open invitation. Her interior is jet black, off-setting the ruby redness of her hard body. In awe of her undeniable superiority over the lowly subjects surrounding her, I approach, softening my step in deference to her nobility. Her face is fierce: determined eye-like headlamps softened by a chrome-bumper Mona Lisa smile. Emblazoned across the bridge of her nose are four letters, F-O-R-D. They hover above a modest rectangular grill centered with the profile of a silver horse in mid-gallop with its head streaming forward and tail flowing behind in the wind.

> **mustang** \mes-tanj\ n [mestengo, fr Spanish, stray]: small hardy horses of the American west descended from north African steeds brought over by the Spanish Conquistadors. Thousands roamed the western plains wild until 19th century expansion from the east depleted the herds. Known for its fiery temperament, cowboys often rounded up mustangs for use as work horses. Bronco Riding, a popular sport today, derived from old-time bronco busters who would ride or

"break" wild mustangs into submission. See also **bronco** 1, **pony** 2, **wild horses** 1.[155]

"I see you really know your cars."

The voice startles me. I turn and face a man wearing a polyester navy blue blazer, an olive green tie, and one of those cheap shirts with an indistinguishable ribbed pattern crawling over it.

"You realize what you're looking at, pal?"

"I . . ."

"A `68 Ford Mustang Convertible: a real power-house on wheels for the man that can handle it."

Black hair, pale pasty skin, he reminds me of a 1950s T.V. game-show host.

"This baby's fitted with a 390 horsepower high-performance V-8 that would blow the rear off most cars. But don't take my word for it. Check the engine out yourself."

He leans over the driver's door with exaggerated ease emphasizing the convenience of a convertible with the top down. He pulls a hidden lever and the hood pops up slightly. Removing his jacket with a flourish, he turns it inside out, folds it, and drapes it over the car door. Walking toward me he says, "Now let's get down to business." He rolls his sleeves up, "See, nothing hidden," and lifts the hood.

The engine looks like a confusing jumble of wires, hoses, pipes, fans, steel boxes, and circular configurations.

"See that," he waves toward a frying pan, "still got the original chrome valve covers and air cleaner lid with HI-Po graphics. And check that out," pointing at a steel heart with copper wire arteries, "that's a four-barrel carb for improved emissions. But don't worry, it won't hamper horsepower readings on the dyno.

"This baby is a deep breather, if you know what I mean pal," he winks. "Long on torque and generous in power potential—does its best work in the 5000 rpm range." He shakes his head and surveys the engine. "Yeah, this baby's a real screamer. You like screamers, don't ya?"

I look up and he's looking right at me.

"Screamers? Yes, why of course."

171

"Then this baby's for you." He winks. "Hey pal, want to make her scream?"

"Scream, me, how?"

"Take her for a test drive, unless you got a better idea."

"No, I trust you."

Often needing ten horses for each working cowboy, domesticated mustangs filled up the remuda made up of the extra mounts required to herd cattle. Possessing the right mixture of fearlessness needed to stand up to an ornery longhorn, durability to withstand the rough terrain, and stamina required for hours of heavy riding in desert heat or mountain snow, mustangs were also capable of the quick sprints necessary for cutting off stampeding cattle. Cowboys were said to both respect and identify with the wildness just beneath the surface of even the most domesticated mustang. "A mustang is like a good woman," an old saying goes. "Always ready to leave you if you don't treat 'em right."[156]

The bright florescent office light nearly blinds me as I wait for the salesman. My gloves stick uncomfortably to black leather, but the chair embraces me warmly. I rarely fit in armed chairs, but this one opens wide enough for snug support. It's almost like being hugged. It would make a fine replacement for my old wooden roundabout in the living room. I could put that one in the kitchen, maybe eat there from now on.

But that's all in the past now.

I quickly check the clock and my heart jump-starts. I should leap from the chair's grasp and find the salesman. Visiting time will be over in a couple of hours. I've got to get this wrapped up. But I must calm down first. I search the office for things to take my mind off such worries.

My attention finally focuses on a picture of the salesman with his lovely wife, two kids and the family dog (held by a little boy). It graces a desk littered with papers and thick ring notebooks. Everyone looks bright and attractive in the photo, except the boy who doesn't smile and clutches the dog, a miniature collie, which appears ready to leap off his lap and out of the picture. The girl must be a few years older, maybe seven years old, maybe eleven; it's so hard to tell sometimes. Pictures make girls seem older.

The salesman walks into the office with a computer printout flowing to the floor.

"Nice family."

"The girl ain't mine, that came from her," he waves his hand toward his wife's smiling face. "But the boy, that's mine." He sits sweeping the printout on the desk.

"Nice looking kid."

He looks at me with distrust. It's the most sincere expression, verbal or otherwise, that I've received from him all morning.

"The kid's a pain in the ass. The school specialist says he's learning disabled, whatever that means. Yeah, he's got a learning disability all right—he's lazy, that's what it is! Laziness, that'll disable any boy. Now me, I'm self-made: no father got me a job; no school specialist made up excuses for my failures. You sink or swim in this world. I'm a swimmer . . ." I fidget in the leather chair and accidentally bump my knee on the desk. He turns his attention toward me. " . . . and I can tell that you are too, a real survivor. Am I wrong, huh, am I wrong?"

"I guess so," rubbing my leg.

"You bet I'm right. Now I've got something special for you, pal," he smiles again and rustles the printout towards me. "This is a complete printout of the Projected Cost Breakdown, Option List, Vehicle Service Contract, Customer's Checklist for Delivery, Certificate of Title, Certificate of Origin, Retail Certificate of Sale, 30 Day/1000 Miles Implied Warranty, BMYADACY-KOPEK State Used Vehicle Limited Warranty, Smart Lease Option, Extended Protection Coverage, Vehicle Cash Purchase Agreement or Credit Purchase Agreement with Proposed Payment Scheduling Alternatives, Buyer's Guide, Projected Invoice, Transaction Summary, and the results of the Projected Buyer DMV Search Inquiry. This is just a computer printout so, in itself, it's not binding, but everything here is

100% accurate and truthful in fact and coverage, unconditionally guaranteed!"

I try to fold the printout like an unruly newspaper. I look up to catch him gazing over my shoulder to the showroom floor. His eyes take on the look of a cat's when something rustles in the woods. He stands and puts on his jacket.

"Look it over and take your time. We don't push our customers here. An informed customer always makes the best decision for everyone involved, so," he adjusts his tie, "you look that over and any questions you have, feel free to ask." I look over and see a man wandering among the shiny new cars. As the salesman makes for the door, he says, "I'll leave you alone to read that over and be right back, so don't go anywhere."

Before he makes it out the door, I spin the chair around and ask, "Could you wait one moment, please?"

He pauses, caught off guard by my sudden forwardness.

"I'm very sorry to bother you, I know you're very busy, but I'm ready to buy the car right now. I have the money."

He looks mournfully toward the showroom. The customer on the other side of the glass, now standing still, checks his watch.

"We can wrap this up in a minute, pal, if you just let me direct this man towards a new car."

"I can't wait. I must drive out of here this afternoon. I have a money order made out directly to this franchise. Can you or can't you sell me a car right this minute."

"Yes I can."

"Then let's start signing things."

Reluctantly he sits back down. I get a sense of power that I usually can only feel at home. The customer on the floor checks his watch again and leaves.

To this day, there are still wild mustangs. To witness a herd roaming the plains is a sight to behold. Dashing full speed and trailing their unruly manes, they seem to encompass the soul of the cowboy as well as the spirit of the west in striving to remain free from the reigns of civilization.[157]

"O.K." he says, "Where do you work?"

"Work?"

"Yes, work, job, title, yearly salary."

"I have a monthly allowance."

His face takes on that sincere look again. "Allowance, what do you mean allowance? Like what I give my kids?"

"Only if they're good, I hope."

"Is that supposed to be funny? I'm asking you a simple fucking question."

"Such language!" I feel my power slipping.

"Work—do you or don't you?"

"I work every day."

"On what?"

"Oh, on lots of things. I have a list I can show you."

"But your job, your official title, what is it?"

"I'm the lone recipient of a trust fund managed by a lawyer and a stock broker."

"How much do you get a month?"

"My mortgage, maintenance, electricity, heat, and phone bills are paid for automatically"

"How much do *you* get?!"

"$350."

"What?"

"But I don't spend it all on food, rarely buy clothes and never go out."

He looks to the ceiling. "He doesn't work."

I don't feel any power at all. "I've been able to save a lot of money. I have a money order . . ."

"How do you expect to get credit, if you don't have a job."

"My lawyer can vouch for my voracity. He's an old family friend."

"Your lawyer can't do shit. He doesn't even trust you with anything more than pocket change." He puts his head in his hands and pauses. He must be thinking of a way to help me. "Wait. How much is that money order made out for?"

"$3,691.84."

"Lemme see that." He snatches it from my hand and looks it over front and back. His face relaxes and he smiles. "Have I got a car for you."

pinto \pin-to\ n [pintar fr. Spanish, to paint]: spotted horse so named for its painted appearance. Pintos were once war ponies of the Nez Perce Indians before the defeat of Chief Joseph in 1877 after which their horses were scattered along the northwestern plains.[158]

White with dull stains splashed over its body like spots on a sick dalmatian, the car is wedged in the corner of the lot and looks as if it hasn't been moved in weeks. If I had spent hours rather than seconds surveying the lot before choosing the mustang, this would have been the one car I would have forgotten immediately. Then it hits me, a little moment of truth: inconspicuousness is one of the most important qualities my car must possess if I am to succeed in my mission.

"This baby suits you better, after all, you're no speed demon, are you?"

"No," I acknowledge, "I'm not built for speed."

"It's smaller too, easier to park and think of the gas mileage, three times better than that old Mustang."

"What kind of car did you say this is?"

"A Pinto, a Ford Pinto. A real classic. You must have heard of them."

"I believe I may have, but I think it was in some crash dummy test."

"Oh that. Those tests were all fixed by left-wing radicals who wanted easy money for drugs. They claimed the gas tank was designed wrong, but the gas tank is fine."

"I think I recall reading in the newspaper years ago that Ford was sued and lost."

"They didn't lose; they settled out of court. Ford had to. They were getting reams of bad press. It was a smear campaign for the press to sell papers. This is a great car, a 1980 model, regrettably the last production year. Just give it a knock." He knocks on the hood. "Here that gong? That's

176

American steel, no clang like a Jap car. Yes, they don't make cars like this anymore."

"I haven't seen one of these in years."

"Ah, you just don't notice them. They blend in so well to the American landscape that you don't realize how many of them are still on the road until you start looking for them."

"Can I get in and try to turn the motor over?"

"Sure thing, pal, I got the keys right here. First let me pull that seat back for you if you don't mind." He loudly cranks it back. "There. See, enough room in the front seat to fit an elephant."

I squeeze myself through the door by going in head first then turning sideways and nudging my thighs under the wheel which fits snugly against my stomach.

"Does this chair go back any further?"

"Why would you want to do that? A snug fit is a safe fit."

I put the key in, turn, give it a little gas. Nothing.

"Don't flood the engine now. Try again."

On the third try, it finally turns over. I give it gas and feel the power of the motor in my hands as it revs up.

"Look at that speedometer, just 44,000 miles. A spinster owned it and only drove it to church on Sundays. It's the best deal on the lot, but you got to take it today. I doubt it'll last the morning. The next guy in could be the one to buy it. It's practically a virgin car, pal. You're the first I've shown it to since it came in yesterday and you know how guys jump on virgin meat. Well this baby's hot to trot and her prom dress won't stay on for long."

I feel right at home behind the wheel of this lost classic, this misunderstood orphan of the auto industry. I can feel it in my bones. This will be my mount. My Pinto and I will hit the dusty trail together come what may.

You can judge a man by the horse he rides.[161]

I'll call her . . . Allamanda! Yes, Allamanda—a perfect

name for a pinto pony. Together we'll ride into the sunset,
me and my pinto, Allamanda, on a mission of mercy.

> "I've ridden weary miles with him;
> I've starved and faced the bears with him;
> and I've played the fiddle when he danced
> while a sergeant and a deputy sat in the
> room with orders to arrest him, dead or
> alive."   - Frank B. Coe[160]

Chapter Twenty-One

> "One day, while a half-blind old man was traveling on his burro, Billy the Kid and Sostenes the Bandit rode up. Sostenes said, 'Billy, let's kill this old blind man just to see how old blind men die.' "'Let him alone,' commanded the Kid. 'He's doing no harm.' The old man thought his day had come, and when the kid prevented Sostenes from killing him, *El Chivato* became the old man's hero."
>
> - Guadalupe Baca De Gallegos[161]

I know I should sleep, but I also know it's now or never. I'm beyond sleep anyway. I am not awake in the way that those who have slept *are*, but in the way that only those who have not slept *can be*. Attempting to sleep in bed would be pointless anyway. As soon as I slip into a deep sleep, my instincts shake me awake like a man driving at night along a dark empty highway nudged shockingly awake by his tires rubbing against the shoulder.

With an understanding beyond rationality, I sense that if I do give in to sleep, Morpheus, on his flight to the land of slumber, will simply drop me. Then, I'll sink so deeply into the dark pool of subconscious space that I'll never surface again and drown for all eternity. Some God is plotting against me. (Which God? There are too many from too many cultures to determine, who knows which one I've upset.) Still, there is one way to stop the demon that's been suffocating me in my sleep. Thanks to another God, one who has mercy on my soul, I've been shown the road to redemption. I must complete my appointed task, however. Until then, bed is a place of peril. Out of the corners of my eyes, occasional flashes keep me alert for trouble. I jump as the phone rings. I pick up and listen.

"Hello . . . Hello . . . Hello . . . ?"

That's the last time I'll ever have to listen to that.

"Have you anything to say," asked Judge Bristol, "why the sentence of death should not be passed upon you?"

"No," replied the Kid with conversational nonchalance, "and if I did have anything to say, it wouldn't do me no good."

"Then it is the order of the court that you be taken to Lincoln and confined in jail until May the thirteenth and that on that day, between the hours of sunrise and noon, you be hanged on a gallows until you are dead, dead, dead.

"And may God have mercy on your soul."[162]

The waiting room is empty today as I slide past orderlies loading the wheelchair-condemned onto a medical bus. The laughing lady occupies the front desk. Holding the phone with her shoulder, she moves papers about, occasionally filing one. I walk in as she cackles and spins on her chair to file a folder on the other side. With her back to me I slip by into the stairwell, where safe, I can take a deep breath and compose myself for the steep climb.

Some strange astringent has been used to clean the stairwell which stings my eyes. The two flights leave me breathless. Coming out, I'm disoriented. Easter decorations, sloppily hand-cut, haphazardly line the walls in a Matissian nightmare of cheap pink and light green construction paper. Trying to remember the room number, I follow my nose, figuratively of course because I'm breathing carefully through the mouth. I find the long hallway. Cluttered with abandoned human wrecks and faceless white-smocked orderlies, no one pays me any mind as I walk towards the room at the end. The door is slightly ajar again. I peak inside. Mercifilly, he's asleep. I walk to his bed. He looks so peaceful—eyes half closed, mouth half open—he could be dead all ready, but he isn't. This is the last look I'll get of him, here, in this bright white hell and I'm filled with a sudden pride because I know that I will be the angel of his deliverance, me, Walter the nobody, former anonymous apartment dweller, former beautiful loser, former member of the living dead. Carefully, without disturbing his sleep, I pull the pillow from under his head.

The report of a shotgun brought the townspeople to their doors up and down the street. News about some sort of tragedy at the courthouse spread quickly. Billy the Kid had done something terrible again. "I told you so," ran from mouth to mouth. The desperado was loose; he might be planning other atrocities. Panic fell upon the town. Best for Lincoln to keep indoors. So the villagers, having rushed out, rushed in again, drew the bolts, and closed the shutters. Half-a-dozen men eating dinner in the Wortley Hotel crowded pell-mell out upon the porch. That was as far as their curiosity took them. Enthusiasm for investigation evaporated when they saw Olinger stretched dead across the street. They remained on the porch as spectators, awaiting the next act in the play.[163]

"Great-grandfather?"

"Huh . . ."

"Great-grandfather, are you awake?"

"¿Quien es? ¿Quien es?"

"It's me."

"¿Es Chávez?"

"No, Walter."

"¿Quien es, Walter?"

"Walter, your great-grandson. Walter, the name you've got plastered all over your room, the number you've been calling for days, weeks, years. I'm here. I've come to save you. We're going to make a break for it. You're going to be free again."

"Great-grandson? I have no great-grandson. Had a grandson though. Up and died in a motor car accident with his wife. His wife—a fine looking filly, she was."

"We're making a break for it, Great-grandfather. Are you game?"

His eyes light up. "Am I game? Am I game! Ain't never been a man more game than me." His brows furrow in confusion. "What's all this talk about a game?"

"Do you want to break out of here or not, old-timer?"

"Break out! Are we bustin' out of this damn jail? Terrible place to put a fellow in."

"You bet we're busting out. Are you ready to leave?"

"Where's my horse?"

I toss the pillow on the seat of the wheelchair. "Right here, saddled up and ready to ride."

"Good. I'm a little weak from doing so much time in this hell-hole. Help me mount up. Hey wait. This ain't no horse. It's a damn mule!"

"It's all we got, Great-grandfather. Do you want to go or stay?"

"An army couldn't keep me here. Let's ride."

He tries to roll over, but is held back by his left arm still shackled to the bed. My heart leaps into my mouth. How could I have forgotten?

"Looks like I'll have to slip this cuff," he remarks.

"But how?"

"Folding-palm technique—watch."

Using his right hand, he folds his left palm inward and miraculously slips out.

"Ha! Never was a shackle made that could hold me."

He rolls over but can't get up. I have to help him—another part I hadn't thought out. He seems as fragile as a boiled chicken wing. I'm afraid to touch him. He puts his right arm around my shoulders. His touch is clammy and ice-cold.

"What are you waiting for? You some kind of greenhorn? Swing my legs out."

I hesitate.

"Are you getting paid in Arbuckle stamps? Drag my legs over the edge, pronto!"

I obey.

"Now lift me up and don't drop me."

Even though he looks light, he seems to weigh a ton. When I finally have him in the air, I realize the wheelchair is facing the wrong way.

"What's holding your jerk line, son, got teeth in your saddle?"

I try to maneuver the wheelchair around, but shifting all the weight to one foot throws my balance off. My muscles begin to quiver. My back spasms and bends like a pencil ready to snap. With a last grunt, I toe the wheelchair. It spins around just as he slips off my shoulder. I lean his fall toward the chair and it catches him with a loud clang.

"Jesus-Lord have mercy, you want me to shake hands with St. Peter?"

An overwhelming dizziness flushes over me and I feel a chill like diving into a cool pool bathed in sweat. I lean against the bed, heart pounding, then sit. The bed sinks like a trampoline. I've just begun the long journey and I'm already too tired to continue. I turn toward my great-grandfather slumped in the wheelchair and mercifully he's asleep —or is he? Hands shaking, I check his neck for a pulse. Where's the jugular? I find it. He's alive, just sleeping. Morpheus has finally come to my aid. I must move him before he wakes.

By Gods, I almost forgot the $100,000 underwear.

The front door in the second story of the courthouse opened. Out upon the porch high above the street stepped Billy the Kid. He still wore his leg irons, but the handcuffs had disappeared from his wrists; he had slipped them off without great difficulty over his remarkably small hands. The sheer bravado of his appearance was his gesture of drama. It made him a target for death from a dozen places of concealment; but no hidden foe ventured a shot to avenge Olinger and Bell. With the porch as his stage, he stood for a moment leaning upon his shotgun like an actor awaiting the applause of his audience at the close of a big scene.[164]

Feedback permeates an announcement from a cheap speaker horn, "Easter dinner will be served at 5:45 sharp. Those who have requested room service must fill out their meal ticket by 12:30 in order to receive dinner. No ticket will be accepted after that time. This announcement will not be repeated."

With his lap full of old boxer shorts, no one seems to notice us as I roll him down the hall. Light blue orderlies go about their business pushing carts with breakfast trays stacked on top and steel potty pans below. Some, with rough nonchalance, pull stretchers with swinging I.V. units jabbed into pale yellow arms. A young man and woman talk, smiling and laughing as if they were in the park on a picnic rather than at work surrounded by the rotting flesh of dumped grandpappies and grannies wheezing last gasps of germ-infested air. Lying in helpless heaps beneath starch-stiff sheets, they're like iced-souls in Dante's ninth. Clouded eyes, frozen open, transfix upon the fluorescent phosphorescence swirling above. Reaching into the smoky hue of fogged memory, a flaccid arm grasps the air as fading faces of youth circle above in a mad dance of projected phantoms.

As we pass by, I feel heads turn and eyes clawing me and it takes all my energy to keep from shivering uncontrollably, but I don't dare look behind for fear of being dragged back into Hades. Why doesn't anyone say anything? Are they waiting to nab me outside as soon as I pass the final threshold?

Great-grandfather wakes up and demands, "Where am I?"

An elevator opens just in time.

Billy then addressed his audience watching intently from across the street on the porch of the Wortley hotel. "I have command of eight revolvers,

184

six rifles, and this here shotgun courtesy of Bob Olinger who you see before you. When I grabbed Bell's revolver, I told him that I intended only to lock him in the armory, but he ran and I had to kill him. I do not wish to kill anyone else, but I'm standing pat against the world and if anyone interferes with my escape I shall be forced to shoot him dead."

Godfrey Gauss, the fatherly, white bearded German who was once the cook at the Tunstall ranch, had been standing there stunned before Olinger's riddled corpse. He was about to turn and run when he heard the Kid's voice stopping him in his tracks.

"Don't run, Gauss. I'd never hurt you old man. I will clear out as soon as I free myself of these shackles. Pitch me up that old pick-axe lying out there and while I loosen these shackles from my legs, I want you to fetch Billy Burt's pony from the pasture out back and saddle him."[165]

The lobby is busy now and I pass through with ease as Great-grandfather sleeps peacefully, but outside, it darkens as if ready to rain. Great Zeus, please hold back the lightning! The doors present a formidable obstacle. I try to back out by propping the door open with my leg as I pull the wheelchair through. Stretching as far as I can without moving my leg, I give the chair a last pull before releasing the door, but the door swings violently, closing too quickly for the tip of Great-grandfather's foot to clear.

"Owwwww!"

The desk nurse jerks her head. Orderlies turn. The waiting room goes silent as faces pop up from magazines.

I rush Great-grandfather howling to the Pinto as countless eyes aim a fusillade at my back.

Saddling the black pony proved difficult for Gauss. The kindly cook was old and stiff and the pony, young and skittish. Meanwhile back at the courthouse, Billy gave up after painfully breaking off one leg iron. Tucking the loose end of the chain into his waistbelt, he stepped back out on the porch with two pistols, two fully loaded cartridge belts, a Winchester carbine, and Olinger's shotgun. He sat down, leaned back and coolly rolled a cigarette. He paused from smoking to entertain his audience with songs and jokes while waiting patiently for Burt's pony and even rose to dance a jig or two when the spirit moved him.

> When Billy comes marching home again,
> hurrah, hurrah,
> We'll give him a hearty welcome then,
> hurrah, hurrah,
> The men will cheer and the boys will shout,
> the good town ladies will all turn out,
> and we'll all feel gay when
> Billy comes marching home.

"Hey," shouted the Kid to his Wortley porch audience, "did you hear the saying: a fool for luck and a poor man for children? Well, Pat Garrett takes them all in, ha, ha!"

> Green grow the lilacs all sparkling with dew,
> I'm lonely my darling since parting with you,
> But by our next meeting I'll hope to prove true,
> and change the green lilacs to the Red, White, and Blue.

After an hour, the pony finally grew bored with the game and gave in to Gauss. When he brought the horse around, he apologized to Billy for taking so long.

"No bother, Grandpa" replied the Kid smiling. "I'm in no hurry."

On passing the body of Bell, the Kid said, "I'm sorry I had to kill you, but it couldn't be helped." Then smashing Olinger's shotgun in two, he threw it on the mangled corpse. "You can take that to hell with you; you will hound me with it no longer." Then he leaned over and took a gold watch and fob from the corpse's waist. "This can go to hell with me." When he mounted the small horse with his load of weapons and heavy chain, the pony bucked sending Billy sprawling to the ground, but nobody in the audience dared to   laugh as Billy rose quickly, Winchester cocked and level. He called one of the Wortley gallery to fetch the horse, an order promptly followed, and remounted. Before riding off into the sunset, his last words were, "Tell Billy Burt I will send his horse back to him." Sure enough, to most everyone's surprise, the pony arrived at the Lincoln courthouse the next morning, safe and sound, trailing its long lariat.[166]

I fumble keys and finally find the one for the passenger door, but it doesn't open. The lock turns but the door latch fails to pop up. In the meantime, Great-grandfather has turned his attention from his pained foot to attempting to free himself from the chair's grip, but can't raise himself from the saddle. None of the keys budge the passenger door so I must chance leaving him. Rushing around the back, I bang my injured knee on the bumper and limp to the driver's door. Spying Great-grandfather's wheelchair shifting on the slight hill, I frantically try keys until one works. No time to lose. I swing the door open and hurl my weight through scraping my body along the steering wheel. I reach out, and bearly touch the passenger latch. With one last push, I rock my weight forward enough to lift the latch as a searing pain runs up my left side. I look up and see Great-grandfather's head floating passed the side windows. The hill! Bruising every vulnerable part of my body, I jostle myself back out and stumble to the back of the Pinto just in time to catch the wheelchair before it rolls down Independence Avenue. I pull him back and pry open the passenger door whose metal has caught on the front panel. Before trying to get him in, I lift a handful of underwear from his lap.

"Hey you!"

My heart jumps into my mouth. Still clutching his underwear, I look up to see a guard standing at the entrance.

"What are you doing there?"

"I'm bringing Great-grandfather home for his birthday," and to my amazement the man just stands there. I toss the underwear in back and try to lift Great-grandfather from the chair, but he resists me with a sudden source of superhuman strength.

The guards yells, "Hey you, hold on a minute now."

"Great-grandfather!"

He looks up to me his eyes flaring.

"*Amigo*," I say, "This is *Chávez*. Do you want to escape from jail or go back to that hell-hole for the rest of your life?"

"*¡Chávez!*"

"Let me help you *El Chivato*. You are weak from the rotten food they have fed you all these years."

"*Chávez*, I knew you'd come."

Smiling with toothless glee, he puts an arm on my shoulder and finds enough strength to help me get him in.

The guard shouts, "Hey, I said wait!"

I kick the wheelchair away, rush around to the other side, and wedge myself between the steering wheel and driver's seat.

"Stop, I said, Stop!"

My right glove gets caught on the windshield wiper lever and I drop the keys. Frantically, I rip the glove off and search for the key ring. I locate it but bump the back of my head on the steering wheel. I jam the keys into the ignition and, miraculously, the motor starts right up. Helios smiles upon us as the sun suddenly breaks out from the clouds and shines off Allamanda's dappled hood.

"Giddiyap," Great-grandfather yells.

I slip it into drive and spin the wheels before jerking into traffic without looking. A bus screeches to a halt directly behind us and I hear the crunch of metal as cars plow into it, but there's no time to look back. We rumble beneath the bridge, make a quick u-turn, and swerve onto the West Side Highway heading South by Southwest.

ENDNOTES

1. Walter Noble Burns, *The Saga Of Billy The Kid*, ch. 17: A Little Game Of Monte.

2. Burns.

3. Burns.

4. Burns.

5. Burns.

6. Burns.

7. Burns.

8. W.J. "Sorghum" Smith of Two Guns, Arizona, as collected by Geraldine Frances Prescott, 1938, for the *Federal Writers Outreach Program*. As the Foreman at Fort Grant in 1876, Smith gave young Henry Antrim his first job as a teamster driving a mule wagon hauling logs. This is the earliest known reference to Henry William Antrim as "kid." Henry Antrim had not yet taken to calling himself William or Billy.

9. Deathbed statement by Frank P. Cahill recorded by the *Arizona Weekly Star*, August 23, 1877.

10. James W. Boorman, *Real Cowboys Love Horses, Dogs and Women (In That Order): A Dictionary of Cowboy Myths, Sayings, and Tall Tales*. Part II: Sayings.

11. Patrick F. Garrett, *The Authentic Life of Billy, the Kid, The Noted Desperado of the Southwest*, ch. 22: Liberty over Mangled Corpses. Believed to have been ghost written by Marshall Ashmun Upson or "Ash," an itinerant journalist, drunk, and clerk for Garrett sheriff's office, *The Authentic Life* was advertised as "a faithful and interesting narrative By Pat F. Garrett sheriff of Lincoln Co., N.M., by whom he was finally hunted down & captured by killing him." Historians give the book the dubious distinction of being responsible not only for saving Billy the Kid from becoming just a footnote in history, but for most of the false information concerning the "Boy Bandit" repeated in countless dime novels, movies, and even historical texts.

12. Anthony B. Conner of Silver City, New Mexico (collected by Geraldine F. Prescott, 1937, *Federal Works Outreach Project*).

This is an updated revision of the original tape recently uncovered in the basement archives of the Library of Congress. The pauses, interruptions, and natural language of the original interview have been restored to give a more genuine picture of the famed outlaw. Unfortunately, other *FWOP* tapes could not be retrieved at this time and subsequent references to the tapes will be presented as transcribed. In future editions of this novel we hope to present the originals.

13. *FWOP*.

14. *FWOP*.

15. *FWOP*.

16. *FWOP*.

17. Previous seven headlines, circa 1990's, taken from various New York City newspapers, none worthy of note.

18. Steven and David Buchanan, "Billy the Kid: The Early Years," *The Historical West*.

19. Buchanan.

20. Buchanan.

21. Buchanan.

22. Buchanan.

23. Buchanan.

24. Barbara "Ma'am" Jones of Carlsbad, New Mexico as collected by Evan K. Marshal, *FWOP*, 1938.

25. *FWOP*.

26. *FWOP*.

27. Boorman, *Real Cowboys*.

28. *FWOP*.

29. Bob Dylan, *Billy*, from the soundtrack album for the movie *Pat Garrett and Billy The Kid*. Although it is well documented that Billy rarely, if ever, drank, Kris Kristofferson, a rather ragged and old version of the Kid, choose to enliven his portrayal of the boy bandit with heavy doses of liquor and slurred speech.

30. Bob Dylan.

31. Bob Dylan.

32. Marshall R. Nutley, "Billy the Kid, Fact or Fiction?," *The Western Revisionist*.

33. Billy Dean, *Billy the Kid*, Liberty Records. This instant classic is accompanied by a fine video as well.

34. Nutley.

35. Billy Dean.

36. Billy Dean.

37. Donald Clint, *The Lincoln County War: A Narrative*, ch. 5: The Youngest Volunteer.

38. Clint.

39. Clint.

40. Clint.

41. Clint.

42. Winfred Wilson Smith, *Range War: The Settling of Lincoln County*, ch. 2: A Challenge to Chisum.

43. Smith, ch. 3: Enter the Englishman.

44. Frank B. Coe, "A Friend Comes to the Defense of Notorious Billy the Kid," *El Paso Times*. Frank and his cousin George were members of the original Regulators formed to seek vengeance upon "The House" for its crimes against the local citizenry. They pursued farming and ranching interests after Governor Wallace granted amnesty to all those who would lay down their arms.

45. Thomas Milton Seagraves, "Billy the Kid and the Myth of History," *The American Mind*.

46. Seagraves.

47. Seagraves.

48. Seagraves.

49. *Billy the Kid Wanted Dead Or Alive*, Empire Pictures, 1939.

50. Seagraves.

51. *Billy the Kid Wanted...*

52. Miguel Antonio Otero, *The Real Billy the Kid with New Light on the Lincoln County War*, ch. 2 bibliography. The former New Mexico Governor (and grandson of Pete Maxwell's ranch foreman at Fort Sumner, Vincente Otero, who knew Billy well) wrote this book as a reaction to the inconsistencies in Walter Noble Burn's version of events and his research, much of it first hand, did uncover previously unknown details about the Kid's life. He conducted a wealth of useful interviews with old timers that, while of questionable accuracy, provide a real flavor of the times. Although the ex-governor performed a public service in this matter, it is widely recognized today that in spite of his improved version of events, his book still repeated much of the false information and myths concerning the Kid that were already in circulation at the time.

53. Otero.

54. Otero.

55. Andre Vignette, *The Tragic Short Life of Billy the Kid*, ch. 9 An Orphan Again.

56. Vignette.

57. Vignette.

58. Vignette.

59. Vignette.

60. Vignette.

61. Covington William Dean, "The Lincoln County War: It's Role in Settling the West (Part One)," *The Western Revisionist*.

62. Marshall Ashmun Upson, *The Tragedy of Billy The Kid*, Act II. This recently discovered original manuscript of Upson's play was performed at the Abbott Theater in Santa Fe, New Mexico on July 14, 1906, the 25th anniversary of the death of Billy the Kid. Hoping to cash in on the legend he started when he ghost-wrote Garrett's *The Authentic life*, Upson may have also been trying to correct his previous mythmaking by attempting to be more faithful to the actually facts as he knew them now that most of the key players were safely dead and buried. He failed on both accounts. The play closed after one performance. A heavy drinker, he died a pauper of consumption a few months later.

63. Upson.

64. Upson.

65. Upson.

66. Upson.

67. Upson.

68. Upson.

69. Martin Chávez (distant relative of José Chávez y Chávez) based on the transcripts from a 1926 interview conducted in Sante Fe, New Mexico, by Miguel Antonio Otero for *The Real Billy The Kid*.

70. Chávez via Otero.

71. Add Casey, Roswell, New Mexico, 1938 (EKM/*FWOP*).

72. *FWOP*.

73. *WKZY*, "Morning News Update," Radio Broadcast, New York, 14, July 1965.

74. *WKZY*.

75. *WKZY*.

76. Dean, "The Lincoln County War (Part Two)."

77. Vignette, *The Tragic Last Days*, ch. 13: The Flames of Hell.

78. Dean.

79. Vignette.

80. Dean.

81. Vignette.

82. Dean.

83. Vignette.

84. Dean.

85. Vignette.

86. Vignette.

87. Vignette.

88. Vignette.

89. *The Holy Bible: King James Version*, LEVITICUS 16:2.

90. Smith, ch. 11: Exit the Major.

91. LEVITICUS 16:5.

92. Burns, *Saga*, ch. 14: A Belle of Old Fort Sumner.

93. Clint, ch. 18: War's Aftermath.

94. Clint.

95. Clint.

96. LEVITICUS 16:7.

97. Clint.

98. Smith, ch. 12: The Ring Regroups.

99. LEVITICUS 16:8.

100. Governor Lewis Wallace in a letter to Colonel Edward Hatch March 7, 1879, *Lew Wallace Papers*, Indiana Historical society. Can be also located in Maurice Garland Fulton's, *History Of The Lincoln County War*, page 337.

101. Smith.

102. Clint.

103. LEVITICUS 16:9.

104. *Las Vegas Gazette*, December 3, 1880. This is the first known printed reference to "Billy the Kid," who had previously been referred to as Billy Bonney or simply "the Kid."

105. Bonney to Wallace, letter, Fort Sumner, December 12, 1880 (Indiana Historical Society).

106. *Las Vegas Gazette*, December 13, 1880.

107. Seagraves.

108. Burns.

109. LEVITICUS 16:15.

110. *The Man Who Shot Liberty Valance*, Paramount, 1962.

111. *Billy the Kid vs. Frankenstein*, Prince Productions, 1966.

112. *Kid vs. Frankenstein.*

113. *Kid vs. Frankenstein.*

114. *Kid vs. Frankenstein.*

115. *Kid vs. Frankenstein.*

116. Patrick Kennedy of Lincoln, New Mexico, "Letter to the Editor," *Billy The Kid Monthly.*

117. Kennedy.

118. Frederick Jackson Turner, *The Significance of the Frontier in American History*, Holt, Rinehart and Winston, New York, 1962, ch. 1: Address at the 1893 World's Columbian Exposition in Chicago. Because, for the first time in history, Turner stressed the full historical impact of western expansion and how the frontier experience affected American development, this famous essay is considered by many historians to be the most influential of its generation. Turner's analysis of the American mind is still widely held today by both Americans as well as the world at large.

119. Miguel Atanacio Martínez, *Captura Del Chivato Nefario* (The Capture of the Nefarious Billy the Kid), Sablow & Sons Music Publishing, translated by Jacob R. Sablow, 1936. Sablow, a Russian Immigrant, makes a sincere attempt to remain 100% true to the spirit and beauty of the original Mexican Spanish, but some minor liberties were taken in order to maintain a remotely similar rhyme scheme. Unfortunately, this haunting ballad was never recorded, but for interested guitarists the chords are simple.

> Andante espressivo
> Time: 8/8
> Strum: 123-123-12 (down/down/up)
> Chords:
> > A-A-E-E
> > E-E-A-A
> > A-A-E-E
> > E-E-A-A

D-D-A-A
D-D-A-A
A-A-E-E
E-E-A-A

120. Martínez.

121. Martínez.

122. Martínez.

123. Martínez.

124. Martínez.

125. Martínez.

126. Martínez.

127. James H. East, in an interview with J. Evetts Haley, September 27, 1927 Douglas, Arizona (on file: Haley Historical Center, Midland, Texas). East was one of the 'Texas cowboys' Pat Garrett recruited to assist in the capture of the outlaws. He covinced them to join up by fabricating a story that the Kid was in the possession of cattle missing from several outfits of the Three Rivers region which was mostly settled by Texans. After realizing Garrett's ruse, the Texans stayed on to ensure that "the job was done square."

128. East.

129. East.

130. East.

131. East.

132. *Las Vegas Gazette*, December 28, 1980.

133. LEVITICUS 16:10.

134. *Gazette*.

135. *Gazette*.

136. *Gazette*.

137. *Gazette*.

138. *Gazette*.

139. *Las Vegas Gazette*.

140. LEVITICUS 16:11.

141. Dr. Henry F. Hoyt, *Wild West Doctor*, Chapter 7: West of the Pecos, Again.

142. *Las Cruces Semi-Weekly*, April 18, 1981.

143. Hoyt.

144. LEVITICUS 16:26.

145. Sallie Chisum, *Diary*, Chavéz County Historical Society.

146. LEVITICUS 16:27.

147. LEVITICUS 16:28.

148. J. Frank Dobie, "Billy the Kid," *Southwest Review*, Spring, 1929.

149. Boorman, *Real Cowboys*, Part III: Tall Tales, "*Libertad Para José Chávez y Chávez.*"

150. Boorman.

151. Boorman.

152. Letter to Wilfred (Willie) Preston Smith from Frank B. Coe, friend and former Regulator, May 6, 1926. Coe was responding to a letter by Smith who had been introduced to the Kid in El Paso and wanted to learn more, first hand, about the man he met shortly so many years ago, but had left a lasting impression.

153. Garrett, *The Authentic Life*, ch. 5: Slaughtering Indians with an Ax.

154. Boorman, *Real Cowboys*, Part II: Sayings, "Horses" (special heading).

155. "Mustang," *Cooper's New Collegiate Dictionary 1994 Edition*, Timothy Cooper, ed.

156. Aviva Belsky, *The Most Wonderful World of Horses*, ch. 8: Wild Horses.

157. Belsky.

158. "Pinto," *Cooper's*.

159. Boorman.

160. Coe, "A Friend Comes to the Defense of Billy The Kid."

161. Guadalupe Baca De Gallegos, Las Vegas, New Mexico, (EKM/*FWOP*).

162. Mesilla Territorial Court, April 13, 1881, 5:15 P.M. at the trial for the murder of William Brady, Sheriff of Lincoln County. It is worthy of note that the court had to appoint a lawyer to defend the alleged leader of an army of outlaws, because Billy had no money to hire one for himself. The lawyer hired to defend Billy, Colonel Albert Jennings Fountain, was a friend of both Judge Bristol and Sheriff Brady, the murdered man. Along with S.B. Newcomb, the prosecuting attorney; Thomas B. Catron, Head of the Sante Fe Ring; and James J. Dolan, the Ring's operative in Lincoln County; all six were members of the same Masonic lodge. Of all the murders and outrages committed during the Lincoln County War (50 men had been indicted), Billy was the only individual not given amnesty.

163. Burns, *Saga*, ch. 17.

164. Burns.

165. Waldo Thomas Flayderman, *Billy The Kid's Last Ride*, Western Adventures Library.

166. Flayderman.

BIBLIOGRAPHIC SOURCES

BOOKS

Belsky, Aviva, *The Most Wonderful World of Horses*, Van Taylor Press, Brooklyn, New York, 1986.

Burke, Sir Laurence, *Burke's Genealogical and Heraldic History of Peerage Baronetage Knightage 1826*, Shaw Publishing Company, London, England, 1954 reprint.

Burns, Walter Noble, *The Saga of Billy the Kid*, Doubleday, NewYork, 1925.

Boorman, James W., *Real Cowboys Love Horses, Dogs and Women (In That Order): A Dictionary of Cowboy Myths, Sayings and Tall Tales*, Country Mud Press, Syracuse, New York, 1983.

Clint, Donald, *The Lincoln County War: A Narrative*, University of Roswell Press, New Mexico, 1989.

Coe, George, *Frontier Fighter,* University of New Mexico Press, Albuquerque, New Mexico, 1951.

Gordon, Andrew, (ed.) *Federal Writers Outreach Program of 1936-38*, Our America Publications, Bronx, New York, 1990.

Cooper, Timothy, (ed.) *Cooper's New Collegiate Dictionary 1994 Edition*, Kabuki Press, Bronx, New York, 1994.

Flayderman, Waldo Thomas, *Billy the Kid's Last Ride*, Western Adventure Library, Vol XIV, No. 2, New York, 1912.

Fulton, Maurice Garland, *History of the Lincoln County War*, ed. Robert N. Mullin, University of Arizona Press, Tucson, 1968.

Garrett, Patrick, *The Authentic Life of Billy the Kid, The Noted Desperado of the Southwest*, New Mexican Printing and Publishing Company, 1882.

The Holy Bible, King James Version (The Old Testament), American Bible Society, New York.

Hoyt, Dr. Henry F., *Wild West Doctor*, American Frontier Press, New York, 1929.

Smith, Winfred Wilson, *Range War: The Settling of Lincoln County,* University of Roswell Press, New Mexico, 1991.

Otero, Miguel Antonio, *The Real Billy the Kid with New Light on the Lincoln County War*, Rufus Rockwell Wilson Inc., New York, 1936.

Vignette, Andre, *The Tragic Short Life of Billy the Kid*, Las Cruces Press, New Mexico, 1939.

NEWSPAPERS

Arizona Weekly Star, Tucson, August 23, 1877.
El Paso Times, Texas, September 26, 1923.
Las Cruces Semi-Weekly, April 18, 1881.
Las Vegas Gazette, New Mexico, December 3, 13, 28, 1880.
Lincoln County Leader, New Mexico, January 15, 1890.
New York Post, 1992-4 conclusive.
New York Daily News, 1993-4 conclusive.

MAGAZINES

Buchanan, Steven and David, "Billy the Kid: The Early Years," *The Historical West*, Winter, 1988.
Dobie, Frank J., "Billy the Kid," *Southwest Review*, Spring,1929.
Dean, James William, "The Lincoln County War: It's Role in Settling the West," *The Western Revisionist*, Part One, Vol. 22, No. 3 and Part Two, Vol 22, No. 4 (1983).
Kennedy, Patrick, "Letter to the Editor," *Billy the Kid Monthly*, Vol. XXIV, No. II (1971).
Nutley, Marshall R., "Billy the Kid: Fact or Fiction?" *The Western Revisionist*, Vol. 29, No. 2 (1990)
Seagraves, Thomas Milton, "Billy the Kid and the Myth of History," *The American Mind*, Vol. 48, No. 2 (1986).

MOVIES

Billy the Kid vs. Frankenstein, Prince Productions, 1966, 80 minutes, color.
Billy the Kid Wanted Dead or Alive, Empire Pictures, 1939, 76 minutes, black and white.
The Man Who Shot Liberty Valance, Paramount, 1962, 122 minutes, black and white.
Pat Garrett and Billy the Kid, M-G-M, 1973, 106 minutes, color.

MUSIC

Dean, Billy, *Billy the Kid*, Liberty Records.
Dylan, Bob, *Billy*, Columbia Broadcasting System, 1973, from the
soundtrack album to *Pat Garrett & Billy the Kid* (M-G-M,
1973).

PLAYS

Upson, Marshall Ashmun, *The Tragedy of Billy the Kid*, unpublished
original, Los Alamos Library, New Mexico.

RADIO

WKZY, "Morning News Update," Radio Broadcast, New York, 14, July
1965.

GOVERNMENTAL OFFICES

Robert Rodriguez, U.S. Congressman, New Mexico.
National Archives & Records Center, Central Research Room Branch,
Washington, D.C.
U.S. Department of Immigration in Washington, D.C. & Sante Fe, New
Mexico.

FOREIGN OFFICES

National Library of Mexico, Miguel Alonzo Valasquez, Assistant
Keeper of Records, Mexico City.

MICROFILM

1860 New York City: Wards 1,2,3,4 in New York.
1881 New Mexico: Territorial Census.
    Annals of Old Fort Cummings, Apache Indian Wars, Roll 500-
    30.

CITY & STATE OFFICES, LIBRARIES, AND MUSEUMS

Billy the Kid Museum, Fort Sumner, New Mexico.
Buffalo Bill Historic Center, Cody, Wyoming.
J. Evetts Haley Historical Center, Midland, Texas.
Indiana Historical Society, Indianapolis, Indiana.
New Mexico County Clerks Office.
New Mexico District Court: Chávez, De Baca, Doña Ana, Lincoln, San Miguel.
New Mexico Department of Public Health, Division of Vital Statistics, Sante Fe.
New Mexico State Library, Western History Department.
New Mexico State Museum, Lincoln.
New York City: Municipal Archives and Records Center.
New York City Public Library, 42nd Street Branch.

COUNTIES SEARCHED

New Mexico: Chávez, De Baca, Doña Ana, Lincoln, San Migel.
New York: Kings.
Texas: Midland.

MISCELLANEOUS

Ash Upson letters, New Mexico State Records and Archives Center, Santa Fe.
Chisum, Sallie, diary, Chávez County Historical Society, Roswell, New Mexico.
Governor Lew Wallace papers, New Mexico State Records and Archives Center, Santa Fe.